Train of Blood

R.C. Rumple

This book is a work of fiction. References to real people, events, establishments, organizations, or locales are intended only to provide a sense of authenticity and are used fictitiously. All other characters, and all incidents and dialogue, are drawn from the author's imagination and are not to be construed as real.

Copyright © 2019 R.C. RUMPLE

All Rights Reserved.

ISBN-9781687632296

PUBLISHER'S NOTES

This book is protected under the copyright laws of the United States of America, and by extension, Worldwide. Any reproduction or unauthorized use of the material is prohibited without the expressed written consent of the author. No part of this publication may be reproduced, distributed, or transmitted in any form or by any means including photocopying, recording, or other electronic or mechanical methods, without the prior written permission of the author, except in the case of brief quotations embodied in critical reviews and certain other non-commercial uses permitted by copyright law.

In Dedication

This novella is dedicated to all the men and women who endured the dangers and hardships of the Old West. Most left with the hopes and dreams of a new and better life. For some, things went as planned. For others, they didn't. But at least they left, instead of living in their parents' basements for the rest of their lives.

I also would like to dedicate this to the real Americans, the noble men and women of the many Native American tribes who inhabited the United States long before the invasion of those from across the oceans. They fought a losing battle, not only against the greed of the white man (so innocently labeled "Manifest Destiny"), but also against the many diseases brought from other lands. As we would fight for our property today, they did the same. It is with heavy heart we look at their plight, as it seems to continue even today.

Most of all, I dedicate this to my wife, Millie. For almost forty years, through good times and bad, you've stuck by my side like glue. One day, you'll learn.

Chapter One

This was one time the pain from crashing onto the rocky tundra mattered not. Lying flat on his back, Carter sucked with all his might to draw air back into his body. The fall from his horse upon the rocky turf had been completely unexpected. He'd been half asleep as he rode to catch up with the rest of his family, a few miles ahead, and hadn't noticed his horse tense up as it neared the clump of trees. He recalled it had stopped and he had nudged its ribs with his heels to get it moving again. If he had not been so weary, he would have noticed the animal's hesitation and warning signs something was amiss. Yet, before half a dozen steps had been taken, he was dozing again.

Carter recalled there had been a growl rumbling in the darkness immediately before a piercing roar had sliced through the night. Terrified, his horse had reared up upon its hind legs and tossed him from the saddle. Slammed against the ground, the wind had been knocked out of him. The fifteen-year-old, now fully alert, realized two things. The first was his rifle was in its carry sheath still on the horse, which had taken off in the darkness. The second was the rumblings which had sent the horse running were continuing to get closer.

The boy searched the darkness, trying to identify what he was facing. Could it be a bear, or even a mountain lion? Both roamed this area in great numbers. The beast kind of sounded like a wolf, but much deeper and larger than those he had been in contact with. Whatever the thing was, it had to be huge to release such a loud and menacing growl. Carter's vision, hindered by having only the light of the half moon, found making out any shapes or movement around him difficult. Yet, his ears didn't lie. The rustling of bushes off to the north told him that was where the creature waited.

Fed by his fear, adrenaline rushed through the boy's body. Eyes bulging and breathing accelerated, every hair on his legs and arms raised ... like quills on a porcupine. Scouring the ground for anything with which to defend himself, Carter's hand came across a good-sized rock and grabbed hold. It wasn't much of a weapon, but it was all he had.

A roar, twice as loud as the first, filled the night once more. Tossing the useless rock to the ground, Carter leapt to his feet and took off running in the direction his horse had traveled seconds before. His boots proved they were better for riding than running, as they caused him to stumble over bushes and tried to trip him up as he yanked at the thorns snagging his pants. Faster he ran, his head pounding in time with the beat of his rapidly racing heart—aware whatever was chasing him was deadlier than any coiled snake waiting to strike out if he came too close. Yet, for all his efforts, the footsteps hitting the tundra behind him were getting nearer. Soon, they'd be upon him. He couldn't give up.

Spying the silhouette of his horse less than fifty yards ahead, Carter knew he had a chance. If only he could stay ahead of his pursuer and reach the animal, he could grab his rifle and give himself an opportunity to live to talk about this. What a story it would be.

Almost to his horse, claws raked his back, slicing through his shirt and the tender flesh below. Staggering forward, burning sensations from his wounds shot through his body—much like those of a red-hot branding iron scorching the hide of a calf's hip. Before he could recover, claws sliced once again, this time into the back of his arm and digging deep enough with their curved ends to hook him, halt his progress, and swing him around. Wetting his pants in fear, Carter felt himself in the unbreakable grip of a creature twice as tall and three times as wide as himself. "What is this beast that resembles the shape of a man, but the snout and ears are pointed as a wolf's?" he asked himself, knowing the answer was not his to receive. The boy struggled aimlessly as the creature opened its huge jaws wide and howled an eerie announcement of victory to all the desert animals. Wasting no more time, the beast's head darted forward and clamped its jaws around the boy's skull.

Carter felt little pain as his skull crunched and brain burst, filling the mouth of the beast with a runny goo of blood and brains. What remained of Carter's head was wrestled free of his body by the beast's assault and was tossed aside, rolling to a stop next to a coiled Gopher Snake. A second beast, then a third, emerged from the darkness and took turns ripping and devouring the flesh from the boy's body. In a matter of minutes, they'd eaten their fill and left what little remained to feed the scavengers of the night.

In the morning, a few members of the wagon train party backtracked to see if they could find the missing boy. All they were able to find were a few scattered bones and his crushed head, the eyes still open and staring into space. "Must've been a couple of pumas," one of them said, hoping to find the others accepting his remark.

Not wanting to stay any longer and take a chance on ending up dead like the boy, another hurried to agree, "Yeah, pumas, at least a couple. Let's get out of here."

Of course, Carter's family wanted to bury his remains, but the wagon master refused to let them take the time to do so. "Too dangerous to hang around here any longer. We need to move on!"

So, to this day, Carter's head still sits up there in the hills, staring into the night, waiting on the beasts who ate him to come back and finish the job.

The crowd of scared kids hesitated, undecided on what to do next. Glancing from side to side, each waited to see who would be the first to stand, break away from the safety of the group, and go back to where their family had camped. I found it funny to see the few parents, who had gathered in the background, exhibit the apprehension of being the first to be chosen. There was always safety in numbers, so they had grown to believe. Or, was there?

I had made the telling of the story a routine. Having the title of Wagon Master, it was my job to lead a wagon train across the wilderness. Before doing so, I needed to make sure all understood there were untold dangers they would face, dangers their past existence had sheltered them from, and dangers they might not survive. Life along the trail wouldn't be easy, and the running off of curious young ones was a distraction none of us needed. Not only would searching for them delay the train's progress, none of its participants needed the excessive worry and stress it would bring. Plus, there was always the chance one of the kids would meet up with a poisonous rattlesnake, or a hungry wolf or mountain lion. That would not only be the end of the journey for them, but cause all of us an even greater delay of a funeral and burial.

Yes, it was my job to keep the wagon train moving westward, at all costs. You might call me the "Excuse Killer". Over the years, I'd learned people loved to make excuses as to why we needed to slow down or stop for a while. Wagon trains before us had fallen victim to doing so and left themselves in bad positions when they had failed to cross the mountains before winter. It wasn't their fault, but the blame lay on their leaders. See, their "Excuse Killers" weren't as good as me and let things go they shouldn't have allowed. Most of those who traveled under their guidance never survived the heavy snows and freezing temperatures to accept the fact.

"Now, you all go back to your families and get some sleep," I announced to the group, aware they'd sit there for another twenty minutes if nothing was said. "We've got one hard day coming tomorrow. The last thing you want is to be in need of sleep when we start out. Won't be any time for naps once we're moving. Go on, now, get out of here!"

I sat there sporting my most serious expression and watching the older children stand and pull up their younger siblings. Soon, when the area had cleared of all audience members, I pulled out my tobacco pouch and rolled a smoke. Tomorrow would be the start of another long and strenuous journey—one I had never planned on making. At fifty-one years old, I was taking on a job meant for men much younger. This would be my thirteenth time to lead a bunch of greenhorns to what they hoped would be a better life—an answer to all their dreams and wishes. Most making the journey before them had never found that to be the truth.

Oh, the land out west was beautiful, but the life would be much tougher than the one they had left behind in the cities. There would be days of extreme heat and cold, physical labor beyond that any had experienced, and the deaths of many ... it was unavoidable. The dead would include those attacked by animals or hostiles, those who died in accidents, and those whose life simply had reached God's chosen end point. Yes, God would be there with us along the way, but the door to his office wouldn't always be open.

My last trip as Wagon Master had been two years ago. At its completion, I had debated taking on another one or settling down like a normal person. Weighing my options, I had taken some time and checked out a few parcels of land to purchase. The property had been beautiful—tall trees as big around as a small cabin, snow-capped mountains so high the angels had to maneuver around their peaks, and plenty of fertile flatland to raise some crops. It was land to die for.

I had met and grown fond of a woman, a widow to be precise, and hoped for her to become a part of my life. While awaiting her approval to both the new homestead and my proposal of marriage, her son was caught by the town sheriff for being involved in a gold claim scheme. He and a few others had worked to bilk the newly arrived greenhorns out of their money by selling them claims to played-out mines. One thing led to another and lawyer's fees mounted. Soon, my donations had made the worthless lawyers rich and me too poor to buy anything. Her son still ended up in prison. When the remainder of my savings had run out, she had done the same. Didn't take me long to figure out she was better at getting money from a person than her son.

Since then, I'd had several offers to bring smaller wagon trains out west but held out until I got the big one. This was no twenty or thirty wagon job, but one having over a hundred and twenty wagons. The money I would make off this one job would put me back in financial shape to buy the land I wanted. Only this time, the land would come first, and then the woman. At least I'd have one of them to show for my efforts, in the end.

With the cigarette burning down to the tips of my fingers, I flicked off the hot ash and put the remaining tobacco back in my pouch. I figured this to be a long trip and saving a little from each smoke might just give me another or two to enjoy during hard times. Funny, this was just one of the strange habits I'd formed over the years to make crossings easier.

I woke at the break of dawn. There were a few moving about, but most were still in their lands of slumber, snoring away. My two assistant wagon masters, Jess McFarland and Seth Johnson, were already standing by the fire and getting the night chill out of their bones, while drinking the day's first cup of coffee.

"Good to see you up, Boss," Jess shouted out, not worried about being quiet. He'd been with me on five previous crossings and, by all rights, should be a wagon master himself. Yet, every time I would ask if he wanted me to recommend him for a job, he'd hee-haw about how it was easier to work for me than to run one himself. I didn't mind. He was my right-hand man, the one I could always depend upon, if he wasn't in the arms of a good-looking "single" woman. He wouldn't touch a married one, but Jess never hesitated to cast his good looks and charm in the direction of widows and daughters. "It's about time to get moving. You want Seth and me to roust up the others? Most will sleep until noon if we don't."

"Time to do just that," I acknowledged, liking the fact he had taken the initiative to think ahead. "Tell 'em we leave in an hour. If they don't want to be left behind, they need to be ready to move out."

15

Watching the two ride off, I grabbed a spare cup and swished the bottom of the pot around before pouring what was left into the tin. It was as bitter as I remembered campfire coffee tasting and I damn near choked on the coffee grounds the two had left me. They were probably laughing about sticking me with the bottom of the pot as they rode off. Served me right for sleeping late.

"They gotcha this time, Grant, didn't they?"

The gruff old voice of Spoonman Williams growled out from behind me. Spoonman was my supply wagon chief and management cook. It was his responsibility to take care of our extra horses, make the three of us meals, and keep us straight as we faced the challenges of the trail. He was one of the few old-timers who had made more trips back and forth across the country than I. The trail life was his life. He entertained no dreams of settling down as I did. No, he would continue to go back and forth as long as wagon trains ran across the country. Besides his other responsibilities, Spoonman's primary function was to act as a buffer between the people and us leaders. He was the "go to" man to help them understand why we did the things we did, and demanded so much from those traveling with us. Over the years, Spoonman had calmed many hard feelings before they had turned into disruptive and violent events. And, as if all that wasn't enough, he was always one I consulted when indecisive. His value as a consultant was much greater than his ability as a cook, but we made do.

"Yeah, but I had it coming," I admitted with a grin. "I'll get 'em back for it before the trip's done. Just wait and see."

Spoonman slapped the side of his thigh and let out a gruff laugh, loud enough to wake a prairie dog in the next county. "I know you will, I know it ... you're good at that. Ain't much good at anything else, but that you're good at."

Tossing the rest of my coffee and grounds into the fire, I rose and surveyed the progress being made. The boys had done their job well. People were up and moving about. Many were eating breakfast or hitching up their teams to their wagons. There was good mixture of oxen and horses being used for this trip. Horses were better for speed, but the oxen provided the strength to get the wagons over the steep mountain trails much easier. Most wagons had their extra livestock, varying between cattle and horses, tied to the back of their wagons as they'd been instructed. I'd learned a lesson on my first trip as wagon master, about letting them roam free alongside. We'd wasted so much time searching for strays, the whole wagon train had come close to being caught in the mountains during the early snows. It was a lesson I'd taken to heart and would allow no exceptions.

It suddenly hit me that Seth hadn't spoken a word to me this morning. He had been on my last wagon train and been a real talker. Like me, he was going to purchase land and settle down when it was over. He had selected a fine-looking spread and put some money down on it. But, when he had sent for his family to join him from back east of the Mississippi, they had refused to join him. His wife had found another to lie beside (one with plenty of money) and told Seth to live his life without her. Instead of fighting for her, Seth had given up. It scared me he had done so. The Seth I had known before had been one to face up to adversity and never retreat. His silence today was an indication the "old Seth" wasn't the one working for me. I hoped the new one would work out.

Saddling my horse, I checked off item after item of my own mental pre-journey checklist. The only thing I could think of that still needed doing was the final departure speech. I passed the word to Jess and Seth to have all the menfolk gather about halfway up the line of wagons, stretched out for almost half a mile. Thirty minutes later, with a bunch of scared women holding onto the reins of their horse or oxen teams back at their wagons, I made my speech.

"I wanted to get all of you together to clear up a few things. First and foremost, I'm in charge and will stay in charge during this trip. My two captains, Jess and Seth, will be next in the chain of command. If you have any questions, you can ask any of us for answers. If you have any complaints, you can take them to Spoonman Williams. I don't want to hear 'em."

I paused a second, to see who might be making a comment under their breath after my last statement. There were always troublemakers. They claimed to be experts at everything but knew nothing. If I could find out who they were in advance, it might help me stop things before they got started. A couple of chuckles came from over to my left. I turned my head that way and gave my sternest look to those in that area. The guilty ones quickly turned their gazes to the ground. Those would be the ones I'd remember.

"We're about to embark on one hell of a dangerous journey. There will be times you will cuss me for making you do things my way. I can handle that, as long as you do them. Do them your way and you'll end up dead or causing the deaths of others. None of us will stand for that. We're going to face all types of bad weather during this trip … drenching rains, scorching deserts, and everything in between, to suffer through. There will be an abundance of wild and deadly animals … snakes, wolves, mountain lions, scorpions … all types of creatures that want you dead. Listen to me and my men and you should survive. Ignore us, and we'll be burying your corpse along the way."

Again, I paused. It was so quiet one could hear a field mouse fart at forty yards. *Good! Just the way it needed to be for the message to sink in.*

"There may be those among us who are thieves or murderers. Do anything here and I'm not only the law, but the jury and hanging judge, as well. You'll pay the penalty for any crime, and most of the time the price will be either death or us deserting you on foot, without any weapons or supplies. Stay clean until you get to your destination and then do as you want. I wash my hands of you at that point.

Along the way, we will probably run into members of various Indian tribes. We'll be passing through lands that they've owned for centuries. Be respectful, but also be on your guard. Most will leave us alone, but there are always some who won't. This wagon train is four times the size of most, so they'll think twice before attacking. But being as stretched out as we are, they'll have plenty of chances to pick out the spots of weakness to attack. I'll have a few scouts, as well as Jess and Seth, scouring the trail ahead at times. So, we should have plenty of notice when we're about to run into them. Don't let that put you into a false sense of security. Be alert at all times and keep up … don't drag and spread the wagon train out. You need to keep as close to the wagon in front of you as possible. Also, when camped, don't wander off alone or without weapons. Only fools do that.

20

Last thing … don't depend on God to save you from anything along the way. God's already done his job. He gave you the ability to reason and think logically. If you ignore the gifts he gave you, he'll ignore you in time of need. Now, go back to your wagons and let's get moving."

"That was really good, Boss Man," Seth murmured as the crowd dispersed and returned to their respective wagons. "Think it will do any good?"

"I hope so," I whispered, knowing there would always be some who had to find out the hard way. Seth had seen it on our last time across. Having the unique ability of almost becoming invisible in a crowd, he had been able to lurk about without drawing much attention. One evening, he had caught and stopped three men from taking a jug of moonshine outside of camp for a little party of sorts. They had been headed to a rocky area along the trail, known for providing rattlesnake dens. Had they continued another ten or twenty yards, they would have run right into a nest of the bastards. None would have returned. "Let's wait and see how many we lose along the way, before making judgement."

Climbing on my horse, I hoped we would find they had all paid close attention. At least Seth had spoken to me. Maybe my worries had only been my imagination at work. I hoped so. I needed all the help I could get on this journey.

I dug my heels into my horse's ribs and trotted up the line. It was time for us to get moving. One more trip, hopefully my last, and then the good life awaited. Damn, I was beginning to dream like one of those in the wagons behind us.

Riding up to the first wagon, I smiled and nodded at Spoonman.

"That don't mean nothin' to me," he growled out, knowing I hated being made to do anything for the show of it. "Do what you're supposed to do. Until then, I'm sittin' here and not movin' an inch."

Shaking my head, I smiled at his stubbornness and gave in to his wishes. Raising my arm, I swung it toward the west and hollered out the traditional words, "Wagons ho!"

The sound of Spoonman's laughter, and the slapping of his thigh, let me know he approved. The creaking of his wagon wheels turning gave statement we were now on our way.

If we had known what waited ahead, we might not have been so happy.

Chapter Two

It had been my goal for the train to cover twenty miles a day during the earlier stages of the trip. Traveling over mostly flat terrain helped us achieve that the first day, plus another five to put in the bank. Fortunately, we were able to camp that night at the river we hadn't expected to reach until the next day.

We took advantage of this and topped off all the water barrels we had, as well as letting the livestock drink their fill. The next water lay a few days ahead and the more they drank now would help them reach there, without thirst being a problem. Spoonman had fixed up some beans and salt pork for me and the boys for chow. That night, they went down easy. Over the next few months, we'd grow tired of them and, regardless of their taste, swallowing them would be a chore—it always was. Oh, we'd have ourselves a jackrabbit every now and then, and it we could scrape up a rattler or two if the fixins got sparse, so there was some diversity to our diet. But beans were the main course tonight and would stay that way until we hit our destination.

The first day was always the roughest. I knew the excitement of being on a wagon train had worn off as the day went on with many of the folks. Driving a team of horses or oxen wasn't easy. It took a lot of concentration and effort. Many of the wagons were full of supplies, causing the wife and kids to have to walk beside them. That was exhausting. By the time the day had passed, the monotony of the trail had set in and the reality of having to do this day after day, for the months ahead, had become a dreaded reality.

We were aware that attitudes would be down, and many would be questioning if they'd made the right decision in venturing west. The boys and I needed to eat fast and then mosey around, boosting morale. With each of us needing to hit more than forty wagons, there wasn't much time. We wolfed down a plate of beans, scalded our throats with Spoonman's coffee, and got started. I hit as many as I could but, after about an hour, I discovered many of the folks had already retired for the evening. In fact, too many were hitting the hay.

We'd set up a watch list and handed out copies to each wagon. Yet, many had ignored it and gone to sleep, instead. Rousting those scheduled didn't make us any friends, but I couldn't let them set a precedent. We could have gotten away without a guard being set that night. The territory we were in wasn't hostile in the least. Yet, we knew if they sloughed off now, they'd do the same thing later, when lives were at stake. That was a chance we couldn't take.

While attempting to shield my eyes from the next morning's rising sun, Seth filled me in as to some grumbling he had overheard while he had been on roaming watch. "I came up behind a couple of gents talking about you last night," he started, trying to be as matter of fact as possible. "At first, I thought it was the regular complaining we always hear from greenhorns. Then, the big one, a Mr. Ternam, or something like that, started telling the other one that he should be the one in charge, and if things got too tough, he'd get rid of you and take over. You might want to keep an eye on him. He might be stupid enough to try it."

I nodded and thanked him for the info. At this early stage, I was a little distressed the grumbling had begun so soon. Yet, as there is always one to watch out for, it was nice to know who it would be.

Crossing the river was more of a chore than we had expected. Early rains in the north had raised the water level overnight, making the regular crossing too deep for most wagons to safely make it to the other side. The scouts found another crossing a couple of miles downriver, so we detoured there. Of course, we had to deal with the normal river crossing aggravation. There are always a few teams refusing to enter the water, that must be pulled and prodded. This builds frustration in those waiting their turn to cross.

That's when the whining begins. Like a bunch of school kids who can't go outside to play because of the rain, we hear adults moaning and groaning the same tunes. One would think they would know better. Then again, some of them wouldn't be happy unless they had something to bitch about.

Before we knew it, two months had passed by since our departure from Oklahoma City. We had rolled steadily along, the wagons creaking and oxen mooing, without much to seriously complain about. There were a few snakebites and other accidents to deal with but, for the most part, the human injury factor was minimal. What bothered me more than anything was the lack of maintenance being done on the wagons and causing repair delays. Regardless of how many times the folks were reminded to pack the wheels with axle grease, there were still those who failed to comply. As with all the previous wagon trains I'd led, the boys and I finally had to depend on threats of leaving the guilty ones behind to fend for themselves if they didn't do as told. I always hated resorting to that, but sometimes the threat of undesirable consequences was the only thing to penetrate their hard heads.

Month three placed us just inside the Arizona Territory. From Oklahoma, we had made our way south to the Santa Fe Trail. It had been a tried and tested route for many crossings and was generally the safest. We arrived when planned, but were met by late summer rains unusually ahead of schedule. These downpours hunkered us down in the desert while the skies pissed on us, day after day. Of course, the rains made it nearly impossible to keep any fires going for warmth, protection, or cooking. Cold and hungry, sleep didn't come easy. The growls of mountain lions prowling about, and the howls of wolves and coyotes in the distance, haunted our evenings. Most of us slept with one eye open and a gun cocked and ready to fire, if we were able to sleep at all.

The sleeping arrangements for me and the boys had never been great, but with the rains, they made sleep almost impossible. Spoonman slept inside, but the rest of us had to share space under his wagon to escape the rain. Much of the time we were soaked, grouchy, and ready to lash out at the first opportunity. After a week of that, folks knew better than to direct their wimpy whines in our direction. None of us wanted to hear any of it, and quickly let them know it. We'd survived sleeping on the ground in the summer heat, sharing our blankets with all types of snakes and scorpions, and surviving Spoonman's ever coming dinners of beans and salt pork … but being soaked to the skin and going days without a good night's sleep frazzled our nerves. No exception to the situation, I'd have probably cussed out my mother if she'd have been there.

We were nearing the hostile lands of the noble red men. I didn't hold the same hatred toward them as a lot of men did. It was clear the government was taking their land away from them, acre by acre, and giving them nothing in return. Indians had been screwed over by greedy businessmen, selfish homesteaders, and lying government representatives so many times, trust was a thing of the past. I couldn't blame them for taking a stand. Recently, the Apache Nation had declared war. It was only a matter of time before some of the other tribes did the same ... tribes we could possibly face as we crossed their lands. No, we weren't going to be greeted with love and understanding. I just hoped they wouldn't take all their anger and frustrations out on us.

Our goal had been to pass quickly and unnoticed through this territory, but the rains had spoiled those plans. We had tried to advance, but found progress at a snail's pace as wagons were mired in the powder-like desert soil turned to a sticky mud.

The few times fires could be ignited, the pots over them held little nourishment. We had found supplies nonexistent at the last trading post, where other crossings had loaded up in previous years. Everyone was running low on supplies as well as the basics of cornmeal and flour. Desperate to find something that would feed us, an encounter with a couple of huge rattlesnakes one afternoon during a break in the rain

28

brought a plan into action. Immediately, I grabbed Jess and Seth and, gathering a crowd, we demonstrated the proper way to hunt and kill the venomous bastards. With so many having their dens flooded, they became our most plentiful source of food. And, it was one meal Spoonman couldn't mess up … often.

While we camped and waited for the trail to dry out, I sent our scouts ahead. Information as to what awaited us, both in the way of Indian uprisings and trail conditions, would be essential to continuing forward. Heading into a battle we could have avoided, or onto a washed-out trail, would only cost us precious time and possibly some lives … neither of which we held a huge surplus. At this point, with the lack of supplies, time was my major concern. If we did happen to get caught crossing through the canyons by an early snowfall, starvation would quickly become a factor.

During our extended camp time because of the rains, I'd had the folks form four circles of thirty or so wagons … all close together. No, circling the wagons wasn't often done. It took too much work to accomplish, reduced the amount of privacy each family would have, and allowed the Indians a more populated area to concentrate a barrage of arrows upon. Yet, I believed it would give the folks some comfort, knowing there were others around them to cover their backs in case we did sustain an attack. It was my opinion that the same rains

29

that kept us from moving forward would hinder our enemies. They'd have to fight swollen rivers and washed out trails as we would, and on ponies slowed by the mud, as well. If they did mount an attack, they wouldn't be able to charge in as fast, making it easier to shoot them before they got to the wagons. I knew our foes were aware of all these obstacles and would consider them in the costs of attacking, now. They weren't dummies.

I wish I could have said the same about some of the folks traveling with me.

John Swisher had been a farmer back east. His grandfather had been wounded while fighting in the Revolutionary War for the property they had settled on, and his father had later done his best to make it prosper. John wasn't much like his old man, though. In fact, John had spent more time complaining at his local pub about his having to do the work a farm required, than he had putting forth the effort to seeing it stay successful. He'd dug himself into a hole too deep to climb out of by borrowing money and supplies for his wife and son. Knowing the tax men and creditors would soon be taking his property, he'd gathered up his family, along with all their wagon could carry, and headed west. Running away broke, most of their personal items had been sold or traded off to buy food along the way to join up with us. Unable to stock up as they should have, they were always running short on food and supplies. Some of the good Christian people didn't mind giving the Swishers a little charity, but when their supplies started running short as well, the contributions stopped coming.

Late one afternoon, John was so desperate he decided he would venture out and see if he could hunt down some food before they all starved. So, having not told any of us he was leaving, this idiot had walked out of camp alone. By doing so, he ignored a basic rule of safety.

John's wife had realized long before that the West was a big place, filled with all types of animals looking for a meal, and John would do them just fine. As dusk had started settling in, John's wife, Sarah, came running up to me. "Grant, my husband John went out hunting us something to eat and he hasn't come back, yet," she exclaimed, her voice all shaky. "I'm scared. It's getting dark. Can you get someone to go look for him … please?"

"Why'd you let him go out there by himself?" I knew why she had, but it was a question I had to ask, to make her think she could stop him from doing it again in the future. "There's all types of wild animals out there, not to mention the Apache. Was he lookin' to get himself killed?"

I had almost felt bad casting the blame upon her. Her face had gone blank, not knowing how to respond. She had looked so helpless. "Please, he ain't much, but he's all my son and I have."

It never failed, a rotten man always seemed to have a good woman to hurt, in one way or another. At first glance, I believed Sarah was one of those, and a might pretty one, too. I'm sure she had been in love with him when they had said their vows, but that had been years ago. He'd drug her down with him, causing her to realize life wasn't going to be as grand or secure as expected, especially with their farm sure to be taken from them. Going west probably hadn't been something she had wanted to do, but had no choice. To her, even though John wasn't much of a man, he was better than being alone.

"I'll gather up the boys and try to find him," I told her, trying to sound as if all was going to be alright. Truth was, I had no idea if he would be living or dead, or if we would even be able to locate him with the night coming on fast. "You go back to your wagon and wait until we all get back. I'm sure things will be fine."

There are times you have to lie to a person to make them feel better.

I grabbed Seth and Jess and we headed out in the general direction John had last been seen. It wouldn't take us as long to travel on horseback as it had him on foot, so we figured we'd come upon him quickly. As luck would have it, the rain began once again, erasing any trace of his footprints. For a good hour, we searched without success. Tired and soaked to the skin, we hung our heads and decided it time to ride back to the wagon train. There had been no answer to our shout-outs, and no reply to our pistol shots. Chances were John was lying hurt or dead, probably in some gully into which he had fallen, or had been chewed up by a coyote or two that had caught him napping.

That's when we found him.

I guess I should have said, "… when we found what was left of him." I've seen victims of all types of animal attacks. Wolves will generally tear off hunks of flesh to take to their young, mountain lions will drag the whole body back to their den, and packs of coyotes will eat a man down to the bone. This was unlike any of those.

John's head laid in the mud, five or six feet away from his body, the eye sockets puddled with the falling rain. His neck hadn't been clawed off his body. Instead, he had been decapitated by the sheer power of something getting a tight grip and ripping his head off. Tendons and strips of jagged flesh dangled from nearby brush and the rain-washed remains of a backbone hung from the opening which should have held his head. His other wounds were equally as startling. There were no slashing claw marks, or areas of flesh eaten away by razor sharp teeth. No, this wasn't a kill to feed upon. It was a warning. Whatever had murdered Swisher had sliced his chest open down the middle and pulled it apart, leaving broken ribs jutting up to the sky and a grotesque and gaping hole. I think what got to me most was the drops of rain splattering into an open puddle of blood and rainwater, sitting where his missing heart should have been.

I had held off eating until after Seth and Jess had finished, and was ready to sit down to some beans, when Sarah had shown up. Watching those two puke their guts up at the sight of John's body made me happy I hadn't had the opportunity. I've seen a lot of dead people in my life, but never one gutted the way John had been.

Funny how one instinctively rests their hand on their gun when they see something like that.

"What in the hell do you think did that, Boss Man?"

"I wish to God I knew, Seth," I heard myself whisper, not finding the voice available to speak louder, nor wanting to draw the attention of John's attacker, should it still be in the area. "I've never seen a man killed in such a savage manner before. The brutality of it makes me hope whatever did it is far away right now."

Instinctually, we all spent a moment searching the night around us and praying not to see anything lurking about or coming our direction. We agreed to return in the morning and bury the remains, as the safety of the wagon train, as little as it was, became much more comforting than us three standing alone in the oncoming darkness. Turning to get back to my horse, my toe banged into something metal. It was what had once been John's rifle. The splintered stock had been partially broken away from the rest and the metal barrel had been bent off to the left, making the weapon unusable. Sliding back and opening the gun's chamber, an unfired round fell to the ground. It was evident John had been attacked with such speed and ferocity he had never had a chance to fire his weapon.

There were three things occupying my mind as we hurried back. The first was making sure we were prepared if we ran into his murderer. We had taken turns making sure our pistols were ready and loaded, and our Winchesters out of their saddle slings. None of us wanted to be the next to die. I knew we had each other's backs and would do our best to see we all made it to camp. The second was the camp's safety. I told the boys to check and make sure all the watches were wide awake and standing alert before anything else when we got back. Tonight would not be the night to be sleeping on guard duty. There was too much at stake with a killing beast roaming about. Last, and what I dreaded most, was dealing with Sarah and her boy. Telling her about her no-good husband's death wouldn't be easy. I had never liked how emotional women tended to be, and tonight would be no exception. If any of the womenfolk in the other wagons were still awake, I'd have one of them accompany me. At least then I could leave after giving Sarah the news, and let the others take care of her. It wouldn't be a good scene, but that wasn't the main worry. Here is a woman and a young son, alone in a wagon, heading west. There were dangers ahead I felt needed the company of a man to handle. Her ability to handle a team and move forward also presented a problem … one the wagon train couldn't let slow it down.

As I slogged my way through the sticky, wet muck to Sarah's wagon, I was disappointed to find no others stirring about. Only Jess' cussing broke the silence of the night as he laid into someone caught napping on guard. All else was quiet. I climbed up to the wagon's seat and spoke loud enough for those inside to hear, "Hey, this is Grant. Is anyone awake inside?"

The flap opened and there was Sarah and her son, a coal oil lamp burning behind them. "If you're here and John's not, it must not be good news," she whispered, maintaining a solemn look on her face. "Come in and tell us. We need to know."

Leaning over, I made my way into their small wagon, wondering how my big body would ever fit inside with all the supplies and two other people. I was surprised to see the inside was empty, except for a couple of blankets. "Where's all your supplies and belongings?"

"This is all we have. We ran out of food a couple of days ago. That's why John went hunting. It's been forever since any of us have eaten. To John, it was okay for the boy and me to be hungry, but when his stomach started growling, he decided it was time to do something. John's not coming back, is he? You wouldn't be here if he was."

I figured there was no reason to lie. Sarah needed to face up to the truth and figure out how she could manage to continue with the rest of us. "No, ma'am, John's not coming back. There's no easy way to tell you, but he was killed out there. Some animal got him. We'll go bury the body in the morning. I don't think you need to come along. I doubt you'd even recognize him and it's much too dangerous. Whatever killed him is still out there roaming around. I'll let Spoonman know to fix extra for breakfast in the morning. You and the boy come up to the supply wagon and eat. Ain't no use in you two starving. You're going to need your strength to drive the wagon when we finally get moving again."

Both her and the boy nodded before the knowledge of them being able to eat soon sank in. It only took a short moment for a slight smile to come to Sarah's face. Realizing food was only a few hours ahead, she reached out and drew the boy close, hugging him with all her might.

I found it strange neither her nor the boy shed one tear over the news of John's demise. Although they had tried to keep them covered, I had noticed both had bruises on their necks, as if they'd been choked. I'd heard rumors of him beating them, but hadn't investigated. It wasn't my responsibility to get involved with family squabbles. I had to figure she had stayed with him knowing the price she would have to pay for his love, and it wasn't my place to interfere. I began to regret that decision.

As I turned to leave, she expressed appreciation at my coming by and letting them know about John, and thanked me for the breakfast invitation. There had been no grief, no tears, and no hint of sadness. As I headed out, I had to smile as she was telling her son that he was now the man of the house, or wagon as the case stood. I hoped his future actions would demonstrate he deserved the position.

She had handled it all nicely. I was impressed. This lady was even stronger than I'd imagined. She had taken the news and moved forward immediately. I wondered if this was something she had silently prayed for in the past. Could it be the event had given her the freedom she needed to give her and her son a better life … one without the abuse they had both obviously endured at the hands of her no-account husband? Any sadness lying deep inside had easily been overcome by dreams of a life without being beaten whenever John had taken a notion to do so. Yet, I questioned how long her strength would hold up when she realized we still had a long way to travel, and it would be up to her to keep the wagon moving.

Shaking my head as I walked away, I was glad to be finished with giving the news and moved on to my other priorities. I needed to check-in with Jess and Seth and find out how many of the guards had been alert and ready to protect us from any type of attack. I also wanted to know who I needed to chastise in the morning about thinking they could ignore that responsibility. Still soaking wet from the ever-falling rain, changing into some dry clothes was next on my agenda to accomplish. They wouldn't stay dry for long, but even a few minutes would be a Godsend. Yawning, I suddenly realized how exhausted I was. Yet, any possibility of sleep would only come after waking up Spoonman and informing him to expect two more guests for breakfast.

He wasn't going to be happy. It was going to be a long night.

Chapter Three

"She sure doesn't seem like a grieving widow to me," Spoonman whispered under his breath, frowning as he watched both Sarah and her son empty a plate of beans and help themselves to another serving. "Both her and the boy got too good of appetites to be feeling sorry about him being dead. They were already here, waiting to eat, when I got up this morning. Kept asking me if they could help … like a young one watching his mother make cookies or something, barely able to hold back until she was done. I told 'em both to get back and quit drooling."

"If I'm lucky, they'll eat my portion, as well," I replied with a sarcastic grin, hoping the two sitting a few yards away didn't overhear. "They haven't eaten a thing for a couple of days or more. You know they have to be starving to gorge down the food you cook."

"You ain't losing much weight," he grumbled, while giving my stomach a long stare. "Look, I was thinking, since my wagon is still over half-full of supplies, it would make sense to put a lot of them in their wagon. That way, as long as we're dealing with the rains coming down the way they are, at least you or one of the boys could stay dry and sleep inside with me."

The idea of staying dry was appealing, but sleeping in the same wagon with Spoonman wasn't on my bucket list. Since the only washing he had been known to do was that of the dishes, he was known to carry a personal odor that would knock a buzzard off the corpse of a dead cow. Still, some of what he had said did make sense. "Why, you old softie … you do have a heart. Damn, I would never have guessed. But, believe it or not, I agree with you. I'm thinking we bring her wagon up right behind yours as we move on. That way, you can make sure she is keeping up. And, when we stop for the day, she will be right there to help you with the cooking. God knows it needs a female touch, or something more than what you offer it. Plus, she'll be earning her keep. Even the boy can help you gather firewood and clean up a bit."

Spoonman agreed to my idea without much of an argument. Of course, in typical Spoonman fashion, he gruffly demanded I know he would not be a nursemaid, but more of an overseer. It was a minor point, but I let it go and gave in to his wishes. Not having to worry about them would help me out in a tremendous way. If he had known that, he would have given me more of a battle, just for kicks.

The burial duty for Sarah's husband was on the agenda right after breakfast. I figured the shock of seeing his body was over, and if we could handle this food, we could handle anything. As if God was playing a nasty joke on us, just as the boys and I got our plates full, the rain started falling. Hurrying, we forced down the same mix of beans we'd eaten for weeks, doing our best to fill our stomachs without tasting what we chewed. I'd almost finished when a soft voice sang out behind me.

"I need to thank you for your kindness to Kincaid and me," Sarah spoke as her strong hand lay softly on my shoulder. "Spoonman told me about your plans for us. This is more than I ever could have expected. The boy and I will work hard, and I promise we'll do our best to not slow up the wagon train's progress. I'm tougher than I look, and so is Kincaid."

Swallowing the last bite of beans without much chewing, I struggled to clear my throat in order to speak, "If you can make these beans taste any better than what Spoonman does, we'll be the ones grateful."

The arrival of a gleam in her eyes and a wide smile made me realize how damn pretty this woman was. That damn little Cupid bastard had shot me with an arrow and had melted my heart faster than a rattlesnake's strike. It was the damnedest thing. I was riding out to bury her husband in a few minutes, and here I was falling in love. I fought the urge to reach out and take Sarah in my arms, holding her body firmly against my own. My God, what a scene that would have created!

"I think I might be able to do that, if you will spare one of your men later today," she chuckled, her eyes never leaving mine. "There are some herbs and spices that grow around here. Adding those to the beans could make them taste entirely different. But, as you can see by the way Kincaid and I ate, we weren't disappointed in the way Spoonman prepared them. Still, I'll see what I can do. There's more than one way to repay the kindness you've shown us."

Damn woman made me feel like a schoolboy talking to a girl for the first time and not knowing what to do next. There was a long silence as we gazed into each other's eyes. I almost reached for her hands, to hold them in mine, but thought better of it. Yet, if I had been a gambling man, I'd have wagered she wanted me to do that and more.

"Hey, Boss Man, you going to stand there all day? We need to go out and do some digging."

Jess's words immediately erased the smile on Sarah's face. The reality of her husband lying dead and waiting to be buried reminded her it was a time to grieve, not flirt. Any respectable woman would be ashamed of herself. Then again, most respectable women hadn't been abused the way she had.

As she turned to go back to her wagon, I watched as Kincaid fell in alongside her. Without breaking pace,

Sarah put her arm around his shoulders and gave him a
little squeeze. I admired her tenacity in being able to
move forward, knowing life was going to be hard for a
while. I also guessed she would provide a good rock for
the boy to lean upon when things didn't go their way.
She was a fine woman.

"You're getting a might bit attached, aren't you?"
Jess added as I took the reins to my horse from him and
mounted up. "Gotta say, you ain't wastin' any time.
Afraid one of the other menfolk riding with us will get
her first?"

"You want to dig the grave all by yourself?" I
growled out, giving my best impression of Spoonman.
Kicking my heels into the ribs of my horse, we trotted
off with Jess and Seth laughing and following at what
they envisioned to be a safe distance.

We came upon John's body shortly thereafter.
Sometime during the night, another animal, probably a
coyote or two, had feasted. Most of the entrails had been
devoured, along with what flesh could be stolen away
through the ripped sleeves of his shirt. His head still sat
where it had been the night before—a few insects
swimming around in the puddles of rain in his eye
sockets.

*He looks like he's watching the bugs swim. Damn,
this trip is beginning to get to me.* I shook my head,

realizing how our brains play tricks on us in times of stress. In facing the most hideous of sights, it presents us with a strange viewpoint for humor, to relieve the tension. Either that, or I was on my way to retiring in an insane asylum.

We found a shallow gully nearby and tossed the pieces of his remains into it. Seth tried positioning the head where it was supposed to be, but the damn thing kept trying to roll back away from the torso. Fed up, he grabbed a couple of small rocks to place against the back of the skull and propped it in place. We shoveled a little sand and dirt over the body as a formality. We knew the scavengers would find it, no matter how deep it was buried, and time was a wasting.

"God decides when we're born and when we die. He lets man decide how to live the life he gave. So, let God be the judge of the man we lay in the ground this morning, John Swisher. I didn't have much to do with him and don't know of anything good to say about his life on Earth. Maybe God will be able to find something good to say in his favor if he makes it up there. Then, again, that may be pushing things. Amen."

Every man deserves a burial prayer. What I had offered hadn't been much, but it had been the best I could come up with. Allowing the horses to slosh along at their own speed, we guided them back to camp in yet another downpour. Dodging raindrops the best we could, our conversations bounced around from the bruises I'd seen on his family, to the beast that had killed him.

"No, I ain't never seen anything tear up a man the way he was torn up," Jess hollered out, working to duck the raindrops falling faster than eagles diving after a desert rat. "I don't want to be the one to run into that thing ... that's for sure. As soon as this damn rain stops, we need to move our tails out of here as fast as we can."

"I'm thinking about trying to move forward, anyway," I shouted out, knowing my decision would be a surprise to the boys. "We're wasting time sitting here. I don't want to be caught in a bad spot when winter arrives. If we wait much longer, that's exactly what's going to happen. People are getting mean and lazy, with us staying too long in one place. You can see it in the attitudes of those on guard duty. Complacency breeds slackers and know-it-alls, and that's what they're becoming. It's time to move. I'm going to make the announcement tonight and we'll get on the way tomorrow, at daybreak."

The rest of the trip back was made in silence. Each of us knew what was ahead. Washed out trails, flash floods, rivers overflowing their banks—the trip wouldn't be easy. If we hadn't experienced John's murder, and the way it had taken place, we might have given the rain another week to stop and chanced the upcoming winter weather. The truth of the matter was, we were no longer safe staying put. Indians were one thing, and wild animals another, but whatever had killed John, and the way in which it had been done, brought forth a new sense of urgency. It was best to move on and take our chances with the obstacles we were familiar with and leave the secrets of the unknown to the desert.

It would be a decision many of us would later regret.

Chapter Four

That afternoon, my announcement was taken with mixed emotions. Some of the folks were happy to get moving, others, not so much. Those dissatisfied were vocal about it, to the point of becoming disruptive. I had to get tough and take control, before things got out of hand.

"What do you want to do, take up homesteading here?" I hollered out, after pulling my pistol and shooting a shot at the sky to get their attention. "I wasn't hired to be your damn nursemaid. I was hired to get you to California. If you want to stay, then drop your damn anchors and stay, I don't care. The rest of us will be moving on. After we've gone and you change your minds, you can guide yourselves the rest of the way. Half of you came without proper food supplies, too little ammunition, and bullshit ideas that it was going to be a pleasure trip. Well, I've done my best to keep you alive to this point. It's your decision, if you want to move forward or die here, waiting on the skies to clear up. We're leaving at daybreak tomorrow. Be ready or be left behind. That's all I've got to say."

The crowd, some still grumbling, broke up and made their way back to their wagons. I sent out the boys to see who was doing what, as far as preparing to leave, and wasn't that surprised to find out there wasn't a one not getting ready for the journey. Like always, some people simply like to hear themselves complain.

"You certainly know how to take control, don't you?"

Spinning around, my heart fluttered with the anticipation of seeing the owner of the voice, Sarah. She still wore the same dress, but she had brushed some of the tangles from her hair and made herself look even more attractive and presentable than when we had talked earlier. "They want to be told what to do," I volunteered, giving away a trade secret. "That way, they have someone to blame if things don't work out."

The sound of her laughter eliminated all sounds of wagons and livestock being readied for the next morning. It was a sound I had almost missed out on hearing my entire life. Now, I was addicted to it and couldn't get enough. "Spoonman told me you moved your wagon up earlier this afternoon. He also tells me Kincaid's desire to help is greater than his strength, but that's just his way of saying the boy tries hard. Jess told me you found a few herbs, as well, during your trip into the desert. Can we expect a different taste in the beans tonight? It sure would be welcome."

"My goodness, everyone is sure keeping you updated on what I do, aren't they? Yes, Jess was helpful in many ways," she giggled out, making me wonder if Jess' lover boy tendencies weren't coming out and he was trying to needle in on me, or if she was playing the teasing game. "Spoonman says he's going to sit back and let me do the cooking tonight. I think you'll notice a change. I just hope you like it."

"Any change will be a good one. Another week or two of Spoonman's cooking and my taste buds will be ruined for life."

Sarah was obviously much more educated in book learning than I, but I held the cards in dealing with people. In all my years, I'd never seen a person change so fast in my life as she had done. Where she had been reserved and timid, now she was cheerful and flirtatious.

Questions arose as I used logic to consider what I'd seen from her. I didn't want to be suspicious, but remember, I'd been snake-bit before by a woman after only my money. Was her innocence a ploy? Had she given John reasons to treat her the way he had? Could her flirting have taken place with another, besides him, during their marriage? His being out drinking and gambling all the time would have certainly provided her with ample opportunity to bed with another. Kincaid hadn't shown grief, either. Was he even John's true son? The boy looked nothing like him. Had John only kept the boy as a charade, to keep away the shame of the

51

townspeople gossiping? I knew of people who were self-destructive. They would have it good, and then do something to ruin it. Could Sarah be one of those, as well?

I asked myself, *"Am I self-destructive, too?"*

I couldn't ignore the chance of her being of questionable character. But, in all fairness, I'd been trying to convince myself she was guilty before even hearing her side of the story. I needed to check the saddle blanket for burrs and thorns before judging the horse to be a bucking bronco. Perhaps Sarah's marriage had been so intolerable she had prayed each night for something to save her from it, and her prayers had been answered.

Recalling my military days during the war, the sight of our boys being released from Confederate prisoner of war camps came to mind. Through all their beatings and starvation rations, they had been so enthralled at being released, they could barely contain themselves. Yet, many had confided in me that, during their imprisonment, they'd endured bouts thinking they'd die without ever seeing freedom again. Could that be the way Sarah had felt?

A group of kids rushed by me, shouting and laughing the way kids do. I shook my head, trying to clear it of thoughts of Sarah and our situation. This was exactly the type of distraction I didn't want. It was a short ride to driving myself crazy. I couldn't risk falling any further. I had to stop myself and let the marbles fall where they may. There were too many lives at stake.

I did my best to ignore Sarah that evening and the next morning, concentrating instead on getting the wagon train ready to roll. The time to be all business had arrived. All personal junk could wait. As the sun broke over the horizon, Spoonman slapped the reins against his team's backs and we resumed our trek west. As if God was happy with my decision, he provided a beautiful orange and red sunrise behind us and a clear sky ahead. It was as if he had been waiting for us to get going before stopping the rains. I'm not sure if we were lucky or blessed, but I was happy to take it.

We had made decent progress by noonday, stopping only once to give the teams a rest. They'd been going strong and deserved a few minutes to gather their strength for the deep gullies and ravines (still soaked and muddy) we would come upon later that afternoon. In the distance, I spied two riders making their way toward the train. As they got closer, I could see they were the two Indian guides I had sent out a couple of weeks before, to scout ahead. I was happy to see them. We needed the information they carried. Hopefully, it would be good news.

An hour later, they were headed back out on a fresh set of horses. In my frustration at the news they had brought, I had decided we'd camp for the night right where we were. There was no sense in moving forward. The rains had not only washed away much of the trail, but several of the passes we needed to cross had weakened and crumbled away into the ravines, hundreds of feet below.

This left us with little choice. With this trail gone bad, we would have to turn north and head up to the next trail west, which would cost us valuable time. Doing so would keep us from getting further into Apache country, but put us in a territory even more hostile. Don't get me wrong, the Apaches were a mean bunch, but few in number. They attacked with the "Hit and Run" method … a quick charge to inflict damage and then retreat, kind of like a mouse, nibbling away until it ate the whole thing. Where we were going, the Indians lived in much greater numbers and could engage in a lengthy and vicious attack. Like a mangy cur, they would get a firm grip and not let go. I almost preferred the Apaches.

That was the good news.

"We know you have been attacked," one of the scouts had spoken in a lowered voice, as if it was a secret he wanted none but me to hear. "One was killed and left to the buzzards. It was a warning for you to turn around. If you don't, all will die the same kind of death."

His trembling voice and hand told me he knew something we didn't. We'd suffered no attack, not by any Indians. The only person we'd lost of late was Swisher. I hadn't told him of John's death, yet he seemed aware of it having taken place. "Tell me what you know. You have my ear."

The scouts exchanged worried glances, as if scared to say more or keep quiet. Whatever they knew terrified them … and Indian scouts weren't known for being cowards.

"We hear many tribes are ready for war. They are angered by White Man's lies. Each tribe sent their medicine men and bravest warriors to meet. Bad magic was made and many warriors now can change shapes … become huge, powerful, fierce wolves in men's bodies. One was sent to give warning. You need to turn around, take wagon train back. All die if you don't."

"So, I'm expected to tell everyone we can't go to California because of Indian magic?" I couldn't believe what they had told me. If I went to the folks in the wagons and told them the same thing, they all would laugh me out of the territory.

I'm not saying I don't believe in magic. During my life, I've seen a lot of things that can't be explained by common sense or logic. Preachers called them acts of the Devil, or miracles of God, depending if they wanted to scare a congregation or make them feel good about reaching into their pockets for donations to God. (I bet God never got one penny of any money donated in his name.). Since the Indians didn't believe in our God's miracles, magic was as good a word to use as any. Superstitions revolving around shapeshifting had been around for years, even back on the East Coast. Tribal medicine men were known for giving the young braves some concoction that would send them into a visionary state of sorts. There, they would discover and turn into their spirit animal. It would be an awakening, a means of direction lighting up the route into their adult life. But to create an army of wild beasts was something I'd never heard of happening before.

After sending the scouts back out to check our new trail ahead, I debated on letting Spoonman and the boys in on what I'd been told. They would have to know about the change in the trail we had to take, but the shapeshifting was another story. I wanted to believe it a tale to be used as a scare tactic. Yet, no matter how I looked at it, whatever had ravaged John's body had not been human, nor any beast I had ever come up against in this area. The physical strength needed to rip off a man's head was beyond that of any man's capability. And how else could the scouts have known about his death? If the Indians were bragging about having done the job, and if the job couldn't be done by a human, could a shapeshifter have been the culprit?

Pulling the boys and Spoonman aside, I let them in on all I'd learned from the Indian scouts. As much as we didn't want to believe, we had a hard time not. Still, we had no option but to take the trail through their lands, whether we wanted to or not.

When we had started the trip west, I had planned on it being my last wagon train. Now, with this new danger facing us ahead, it might be the last for all of us.

Chapter Five

The three-day journey to the north before heading back to the west put us deep in Indian territory. I hadn't seen hide nor hair of the scouts since they'd left. A couple of miles after we had made the shift in direction, we came across their bodies.

Both lay in pieces, strewn across their dead horses. The heads of the scouts had been ripped off, but the horses' remained attached. I shook my head, knowing this demonstrated the respect held for horses, and the lack of respect for scouts. The horses would reach the spirit world strong and free. The scouts would arrive, but spend eternity in constant search for the heads they'd lost in this world. Their hearts had been removed in a manner like John's, as well, but with much more savagery. Both torsos had been sliced from neck to waist and then spread apart, much like one pulls the ends of a wishbone until it snaps, their individual ribs jutting out in various directions. The droning of the contingents of houseflies and horseflies gave notice that they had already claimed the bodies were theirs, and to move on. We did.

I guessed this to be another warning. I wondered how many more they would give before a full-out attack took place. The four of us had decided to keep the magical shapeshifters a secret until there was proof of it being true. Yet, all would see these bodies as they passed by. We had yet to see one of the creatures, but we couldn't keep the secret any longer. Lives were at stake. The others had to be informed. Turning my attention away from the scouts, I scoured our surroundings, aware the hostiles could be watching our every move. All those using the wagon train to get to California needed to be on their highest alert to anything not seeming normal and shout out to us at first notice. Otherwise, none of us would escape alive.

Without wasting any more time, I had the word passed for the men from each wagon to gather for a quick meeting. As I took my position to speak, the extreme tension in the group was evident. Rumors of the bodies being found had already passed through the train.

"Okay, let's make this quick. As some of you have heard, the bodies of our two scouts have been found. Before their deaths, they'd told me of the hostiles creating creatures, shapeshifters if you will, from Indian braves. As hard as most of you will find this to believe, I didn't believe it, either. We all knew there was the possibility of running into trouble when we started this journey, but none of us expected this kind. With the death of one of your own a week or so ago, and now the death of the scouts, I must warn you to be ready for

anything. If we are up against shapeshifters, we're
fighting against an enemy so powerful we'd be safer
fighting against our own U.S. Calvary. We'll be
camping soon. When we do, the watch will be doubled.
Any man caught falling asleep on guard duty will find
himself and his family sent away from the safety of the
wagon train to fend for themselves. Believe me, you
don't want to be out there alone right now. So, let's get
moving. There's still a few miles to cover before we
camp."

As the crowd broke up, I could hear bits and pieces of
grumbling. Yes, I was a bad guy who had kept a secret
from them. They should have known everything from
the first moment I'd learned of it. I'd led them into
hostile territory, filled with monsters, without any regard
for their safety. I needed to be replaced, immediately,
and someone with a brain given my position.

I guess you can't please everyone.

There had been a meeting years before, with similar
results. The people weren't happy and wanted to replace
the wagon master for their troubles. I had been his
assistant at the time, and caught in the middle. Yet, I
stood firm with him. As it turned out, he had done all the
right things and the train made it through just fine. All
the people who had wanted him replaced forgot their
words of mutiny and thanked him before he departed. I

talked to him a few years later and asked him how he had held it all together. His philosophy was one I'd adopted, "Fuck 'em all. I know what I'm doing."

He hadn't worried about the grumblers. Instead, he'd faced up to them and shown them up in front of the ones who'd followed them. Usually, they'd tuck their tails and shut-up. When they didn't, he'd either sent them out on their own, or shot them. No one challenged him after that.

I hoped it wouldn't come to that.

Getting the train moving again, all but a couple of wagons pushed onward to put as much distance between the bodies and us as possible. Two families had decided to hold back and bury the scouts, it being the "Christian" thing to do. They were warned about doing so, and told they'd be on their own until they could catch up with the rest of us. Holding firm to their convictions, I pointed ahead to a tall plateau I'd planned on camping by for the night and wished them the best.

We never saw them again. Having a good heart is a tremendous quality. Having the intelligence to make a good decision can save your life.

I was partially at fault for their deaths and would accept that blame. I should have made them continue on with the rest of us. Yet, as tragic as they were, their deaths would help prove to the others it was best to listen to what I told them. Still, those people were dead. They'd made their decision and paid the price. My guilt for allowing them to stay is still making me pay.

With the sun dropping low in the afternoon sky, I put Spoonman in charge, hollered at the boys to join me, and we set out to scout the plateau ahead. The rock formation was one like many we would see as we continued westward. Close to a quarter of a mile in length and width, its sides rose from the desert floor hundreds of feet. The red rock climbed high to the sky, straight up on three of the sides, and had a steep incline on the fourth. The last was where I chose for us to camp the night. I believed it would be nearly impossible for anyone to scale the walls on the other sides, and we'd be in front of this one. By all rights, there should be no way for anyone to attack us from the rear ... or above.

Indians have been known to start rockslides, shoot a rain of arrows, and to throw huge rocks down upon sleeping wagons. It wasn't that they played dirty. They simply did what it took to win. I believed keeping them from having that advantage would be our best move.

Seth returned to the train to guide Spoonman to our spot while Jess and I stood guard. We'd assembled the wagons in a double row, half-moon arch, against the rocks, with our campfires inside. I set the watch up in the outside row of wagons and split it into two sections … one of them until two in the morning and the other until sunrise. I couldn't neglect the men getting proper rest, but I couldn't skimp on having enough guards on watch, either.

"Hey, Wagon Master, we want to parley with you!"

A group of ten men walked my direction, obviously with a purpose. From the expressions on their faces, it was easy to see they had something serious on their minds to be discussed. Jackson Ternam headed the group, with the others spread out to either side of his huge body. His voice was a familiar one to me, as it had been one urging the others to get rid of me at several of our meetings in the past. I expected no different this time. What was different at this confrontation was all the men were armed.

Now, not to brag, but I wasn't a bad shot, nor was I slow on the draw. However, I had no desire to take on a group of ten with one six-shooter. Those were not favorable odds. I needed to think fast and come up with something to take back the advantage.

"Mr. Ternam, I was just coming to see you. We need some watch leaders to keep the others in their section in line. We're in dangerous territory and require responsible folks who can be trusted to help make sure all of us make it out of here. Would you be interested?"

"You know this is a terrible place to camp, don't you?" Ternam wasn't swayed by my offer, as I had hoped he might be. I should have figured that. In his mind, he needed to be the big man in front of the others. "There's too much room behind us for an attack. Any of the other three sides of the plateau have a solid rock facing. We could direct all our defenses in one direction. We want to move. It's not safe here."

Stooping over, I picked up a decent-sized rock and tossed it, none too easy, in his direction. Dodging out of the way, the rock missed Ternam and hit the man behind him. A loud howl filled the air and the man went to his knees, rubbing his leg where the rock had bruised flesh.

"You did well to dodge that one, but the man behind you wasn't as lucky," I shot out, a little frustrated that even my choice of campsite was being questioned by these so-called experts. "I wonder how good you'd be dodging rocks twice that size as they drop on you from the top of the plateau? Camping too close to a rock wall will give that advantage to the Indians. They can't climb up the other three sides, and we're here to keep them from getting up this one. Would you rather face them in your rifle sights from the wagons, or would you prefer them dropping rocks and boulders on you from six or seven hundred feet above? Tell me, Mr. Ternam, I'm waiting to hear your preference."

Boom! Ternam's expression indicated he wanted to say something to have the last word, but knew anything out of his mouth would now sound stupid. I decided it time to twist the knife and make the wound deeper while I had the chance. "Let me say this. You folks are making your first trip with a wagon train. I've been doing this for decades. I know what I'm doing. If you have a question as to why I've chosen to do something, ask Spoonman or one of my boys. I've got too much to do to make sure we finish this journey in one piece than to listen to stupid arguments from greenhorns who don't know their ass from a hole in the ground. Now, you men need to go back to your wagons and get some rest, unless you're supposed to be on watch. If you are, get your asses back to where they need to be. Ternam, my offer still stands if you think you're able to do what I want. What's it going to be?"

The man wasn't ever going to be my friend. That didn't matter. I didn't want him as one. What did matter was getting him to quit being a pain in my ass and just do the job. Nodding his acceptance, I returned the nod and sent the group walking. Pulling out my tobacco pouch, I rolled a cigarette and took a long puff. Exhaling the bitter smoke, I shook my head in disbelief at what had just happened. "Get over it," I murmured to myself. "Two hundred more miles or so and you'll be done with this shit forever."

Those not sleeping or on guard went snake hunting. We needed fresh meat and the rocks behind us would be filled with rattlesnakes and gopher snakes. I had already killed a couple while awaiting Spoonman's arrival. We had been persistent in our training, so by this time, many had overcome their fears and learned how to kill them without getting bit. The closer to dusk the day got, the more they found, as the reptiles left their hiding places to hunt for food. Little did they know, they would become the meal, instead.

There was plenty of dried brush and mesquite around the rocks, as well. Soon, cook fires were burning bright and snakes were sizzling. I looked forward to a meal consisting of something besides beans, even though I must admit, Sarah's recipe had been much better than Spoonman's. Finishing my rounds, I discovered Jess and Seth had already gorged themselves on the stringy white meat. Laughing, they teased me about forgetting to save me any.

"I've got yours right here," Sarah sang out as she brought me a tin plate of rattler. "I tried to spice it up some. I hope you like it."

"Anything will be better than another meal of beans, no offense, ma'am," I sounded out, thinking only after I'd spoken about how it might sound to her. "We all need a change every now and then."

"I fully agree ... and no offense taken," she responded, trying to present a smile, but failing. She gave me a minute to get my mouth full before continuing. "Have I done something to offend you? You haven't said two words to me in days."

I nearly choked. She immediately reminded me of the dance hall girls who doubled as waitresses and waited until your mouth was full before asking you if you wanted something else to eat. It was almost a game to them. "No, I've just got a lot on my mind. This is dangerous land and I've got over two hundred people to protect. I'm kind of busy."

"Good, I was hoping that was the case," she replied, looking a little relieved. "I had hoped we might become good friends ... maybe, even more than friends ... you know ... oh, I better just shut my mouth before I dig my grave deeper."

I kept quiet as she blushed and hurried off. She had been embarrassed, which was could be a sign of innocence. But there were still a lot of questions in my mind I hadn't found the answers to, and I wasn't about to make any type of commitment right now. All my attention needed to be on my job. The other stuff could wait until later, if there was to be a later. Besides, the fried rattlesnake I was enjoying was too good to stop eating.

Setting down my plate of stripped bones , I took a swig of coffee and closed my eyes for a few seconds. I was getting too old for this job. As I grew older, the stress and worry didn't seem to be worth the money the position paid. I recalled the excitement of the early trips west, and how much I had enjoyed overcoming each obstacle I'd faced. Over time, the challenges had become too common and monotonous … as had journeys filled with bickering travelers who always knew best.

I was becoming a bitter man.

Here I was, putting my life on hold, to get these folks to where they wanted to go. They were pursuing their dreams, and I was stuck in an endless cycle. And most of these folks didn't appreciate what I did to make sure they got to their destination safe and sound. They'd get there, find life just as tough, if not tougher, than the life they'd left behind, and fail as they had before. The West was filled with them, failures of all types. I was letting failures change me into the type of person I never wanted to become.

"Do you mind if we talk for a minute?"

Always an interruption. I escaped my world of silent despair and opened my eyes. In front of me stood Sarah's boy, Kincaid. I had never heard him talk. I didn't even know he could. "No, I don't mind. Have a seat and speak your piece, young man."

His flexibility amazed me as he plopped down in a cross-legged position and leaned forward. If I had tried to do the same, I would have torn a muscle or thrown out my back. Watching him take a deep breath before speaking, I realized the boy was building up enough courage to open his mouth again.

"I hate to bother you, sir, but I thought it time we have a talk … you know, man to man." He was doing his best to prove I didn't intimidate him, when it was obvious I did. I bit my tongue to keep from smiling. The last thing he needed was to think I was laughing at him. "Do you know my mom likes you?"

"I had my suspicions," I answered, curious as to whether his mother had set him up to do this. "Say what's on your mind. I don't have a lot of time to spare."

"Well, since we joined up, she's always talked about how much she respected you, and how much of a better man you were than Dad. It really used to make him mad, but she kept doing it. I don't think she was trying to rub it in … more like trying to get him to see it and change his ways. He got so upset one night he started choking her, and when I tried to stop him, he threw her down and started choking me. He finally stopped when she threatened to get you after him if he didn't quit. It wasn't the first time. Once, Mom had to hit him on the head with a fry pan to get him off me."

69

I could hear the honesty and emotion in the boy's voice as he spoke those words. This explained the bruises on them I'd seen. Of course, having failed at his own life, I could understand where her "hero worshipping" and badgering could have got to him after a while, as well.

"Anyway, when you told us he was dead, it was a relief. We had been scared. He had gotten drunk one night when he was supposed to be on watch and promised neither me nor Mom would make it to California. Said he'd kill us before we got there, so he could enjoy the new life without any millstones around his neck. So, with him dead, we were safe. After Mom found out you had set us up with helping Spoonman, and him helping us continue the trip, she was sure you were the kind of man she had always wished to be in her life … and mine. All she does is talk about you, that is, until a couple of days ago. Now, she just cries a lot."

Kincaid's words hit me hard. I now knew, even if she wouldn't admit it, she had been looking to replace him before he had ever been killed. She had to … it was either that or die. I'd fallen right into her plan. Oh, she loved me, but I wondered if it wasn't a fleeting love, until she found someone else who would suit her needs better. Taking the chance to find out for sure was a barrier only time could weaken as trust was built. Yeah, I still wanted her, but to keep myself from getting hurt once again, I needed to go slow and easy—you know, proceed with caution style. Maybe she would be patient and stay with me. Maybe she would grow tired and move on to another. Yep, I needed to wait and see what happened. If we made it to California, I would re-evaluate then.

"Anyway, she doesn't think you like her because she's been kind of forward with you. I've never seen her act this way before. I think she likes you a lot … maybe, she even loves you a lot. I don't know you well enough to know what I feel. This is the first time we've talked. But I know I want my mother to be happy. I've never seen her smile as much as she has the last couple of weeks. It's kind of nice. Before, she was always sad and crying about things. Now she's in the wagon doing it again. Anyway, that's all I've got to say. I'm not the speaker you are. I just thought you should know."

The boy had been speaking from his heart, not a prepared script he had been instructed to repeat. His life must have been the same kind of hell his mother's had been. I felt sorry for the lad, but had to tell it the way it was, and hope he'd understand.

"I appreciate you taking the stand as man of the house and telling me all this," I began, observing carefully to see how he would react. "But I have to say love and your mom are things I can't concentrate on right now. There are hostile Indians to deal with, creatures that rip men apart, a mutinous group of travelers who believe I'm leading them to their deaths while I'm trying to protect them, and at least two hundred more miles between us and our destination. Those all require my complete attention. I can't add my personal problems to all that."

I could see he wasn't pleased with my response, as he continued biting his bottom lip. He wanted something to take back to his mother to make her smile again. I couldn't give him that. "Something neither you nor your mother have thought about is maintaining your reputations. I know your father was a bastard, but he has only recently been killed. This should be a time of grieving for you two. How would it look to everyone if your mother and I suddenly became a couple? Some of these folks would be ready to tar and feather all of us. No, we must wait. Maybe, when this is all over, your mother and I can get together. For right now, I need to focus on my job. Do you understand that?"

The boy nodded, but was silent. He had spoken all his words and failed to get the answers he'd been after. I could see he was disappointed. Yet, he impressed me by sticking out his hand for a handshake. He had taken his role seriously, and was continuing to do so to the end, even though the results hadn't been those he had desired. He was a son for Sarah to be proud of, and would be an even better man when he grew up. That is, if I could find a way to get all of us out of here alive.

Chapter Six

There are nights sleep doesn't come easy.

Doing my best to get some shut eye, I took my spot under Spoonman's wagon and tried to stop shivering as I wrapped up in my blanket. The desert had a chill to it at night, a chill that sometimes brought dangerous bed partners. There was the constant concern of waking up with a rattler lying next to you, as it used your body heat to keep warm. The rocky area we were in was loaded with them when we had arrived. Although many had found their way into fry skillets for dinner, I knew there were still plenty around.

It wasn't just the idea of rattlers detouring needed sleep from my mind. Indian attacks on my past wagon trains had always come at night, unless we were in Apache territory. I'd once heard someone say Indians never attacked after dark. That was an old wives' tale. While the Apaches thought it forbidden by their gods, the braves of most tribes used the cover of darkness, the way many predators do, to conceal their advance. As if this wasn't enough to consider, I had to remember we weren't just facing Indians, but shapeshifters. They'd be faster and harder to see, especially if covered in fur of any type. I just hoped we were ready.

About two in the morning, I gave up my tossing and turning and headed toward one of the fires someone had kept going. I filled my cup with coffee, long past its prime, and burned my tongue taking a swig. The night was quiet, except for the ominous howling of a wolf in the distance and a coyote answering with its yapping. The two animals kind of reminded me of the white men and the red men. We looked alike, as far as our body shapes were concerned, but were enemies. Oh, there were times we tolerated each other but, on most occasions, we had no need of the other and would fight to the death. Shame we all just couldn't get along.

I jumped as a shot rang out and jerked my head toward the far end of the camp, where it had originated. After a second round was fired, I ran to Spoonman's wagon and grabbed my Winchester, before joining Seth and Jess. "Anyone see anything out there?" I whispered to the two, both aiming their rifles out into the darkness. Neither spoke as more shots were fired from the far end of our camp. "They will attack one end to draw our attention, and then come at us from the other. It's an old Indian trick. Stay alert. We're going to have a fight on our hands! I'm heading down there to see what we're up against."

My six-shooter and rifle fully loaded, I hurried to reach those already under attack. The hustling and bustling of the half-awake men, as they stationed themselves in the outside line of wagons, as well as the women opening boxes of ammunition to keep the guns loaded, helped assure me we were ready for battle. If only the children had been quiet. Their shrieking with fear and loud crying drew the attention of the working women, stalling some of their reloading efforts. Again, I was at fault. I had added to their fears before we had ever started, by telling them my tale of horror. To the poor kids, it was now a reality.

"Stay alert ... they're coming!" I screamed out as I passed wagon after wagon, trying to make my warning heard over the nearby rifle fire and screams of those already injured. I loaded a shell in the chamber of my rifle and sent another into the magazine, to give me an extra bullet to fire. I had a feeling I was going to need it.

Flames climbed high from one of the wagons a short distance from the far end. I figured an oil lamp had been broken in the battle ... but by whom ... our people or the Indians? The piercing scream of a child to my right turned my head. There, facing out into the darkness, was the one and only Jackson Ternam. In his outstretched arms he held a small child (one I didn't recognize as his), as if to shield himself, or to offer it as a gift, in hopes they would take it and leave him alone.

I snapped!

Rushing toward him, I raised my rifle and slammed the wooden stock of my Winchester against the back of the skull of the miserable coward. Falling forward, he crumpled unconscious to the desert sand. I grabbed the child and held her, searching quickly for her mother. I caught sight of her under another wagon clutching on tight to her other children and put this one in her care without delay. Passing back by Ternam's body, I had to fight the justifiable urge to put a bullet in him. With regret, I forced myself to run past him and save the round for the enemy ahead.

As I approached the burning wagon, the body of one of our menfolk flew from the flames and landed only a few feet away from me. A quick glance told me there was no reason to waste time on him. He had been shredded ...claws having slashed through his body so many times his stomach and chest resembled a sliced rack of ribs, already cut into individual serving pieces. Almost completely dismembered, one arm and leg lay at impossible angles to his body, still attached to the torso by only the few tendons the attacker had failed to slice. The jagged pieces of torn flesh hanging from where his other arm and leg should be indicated they'd been viciously ripped away.

Before I could take another step, burning bits of canvas shot from the wagon as another shadow burst from the flames to the desert floor, rolling in the sand to extinguish the sparks it had gathered during its escape. Shocked by its appearance, I stepped back a couple of steps as it rose to its feet. Unlike anything I'd ever seen, in front of me stood a creature found only in nightmares … until that night. At least seven feet tall … covered in singed and smoking dark fur … and with the snout of a wolf, its long canine teeth gnashed against a forearm torn from the man lying dead. Seeing me, with its eyes reflecting the flickering flames of the pieces of burning canvas on the ground, its razor-sharp claws clicked against each other as they cleaned and sharpened themselves for more killing.

I couldn't move. I was scared shitless.

Suddenly, the beast raised its head to the sky and howled to its gods above. Chills ran down my spine and held me in their grasp. For the first time in my life, I felt I was going to die and there wasn't a damn thing I could do about it.

Yet, this was not to be the night. For unknown reasons, the beast spun away from me and stormed up and into the next wagon. Inside, guns firing until empty of ammo, screams of men being torn to bits, roars of the wild beast victorious in battle … all filled the air. More had died, in a matter of seconds. If this kept up, the creature would work his way up the line until all were dead.

I could no longer stand still and do nothing. I had to get control of my faculties.

Darting to the area between the wagons, I knelt and aimed my Winchester up at the canvas opening of the wagon where the beast lingered ... gorging itself on flesh stolen from one it had murdered. I knew I had to be ready to fire. The speed it had exhibited exceeded that of a jackrabbit being chased by a mountain lion. Seconds seemed like minutes as I held my position and waited for the beast to appear. My aim would have to be true.

Finally, his body emerged. The barrel of my Winchester flashed, its bullet hitting the beast square in the center of its chest. It was a kill shot for sure, but seemed to have no effect on the monster. As I chambered another shell, the creature arched high and back, preparing to launch its attack. My finger squeezed the trigger and my second bullet entered the top of its neck traveling up, splattering blood and brains against the wagon canvas, as it exited the top of the skull. Crazed with pain, it clawed at its wound. I fired once more, this time into one of its eyes as it peered down to see who its murderer was. His head snapped back as its eye exploded, sending another spray of blood onto the canvas. Now dead, the body dropped from the wagon and lay still, its blood slowly oozing into the sand.

It was a victory I had no time to relish.

79

Shots were being fired in rapid succession from the other end of the camp. *Damn, they're attacking down there now!* Aided only by battle supplied adrenaline, I forced my old and tired legs to move as I hurried back to assist those in need. If we made it through the night, I would be sure to have a horse to ride the next time around.

Three quarters of the way there, the shots ceased. Huffing and puffing, I slowed down, hoping to catch my breath. It was evident my old body couldn't do the things it once did. My legs were rubbery and my arms so weak I could barely keep hold of my Winchester. If someone had jumped me at that moment, I would have been easy pickings.

Still panting, I reached Spoonman's wagon as Jess and Seth were coming out. I worried about Spoonman, but hearing his raspy voice hollering, "I got 'em" alleviated my concern.

"Boss Man, you're not going to believe what we just killed," Seth's voice shouted out in elation. "Damn monster of some sort. We must have hit it five or six times in the heart, but it kept on coming until Jess hit it in the head. That one knocked it back, so we shot at its skull over and over until it blew apart! It was bigger than any bear you ever seen, uglier, too. Looked like a giant wolf, but it had arms and legs kind of like you or me.

But you won't know that by looking at it. We watched it … I mean, we saw it change. It went from a damn monster to a naked Indian!"

Squeezing between the wagons, the three of us crept forward to examine the corpse. The head was unrecognizable—the boys' shooting had done its job—but the body was that of an Indian warrior, not a furry monster. If there had ever been any doubt about Indian magic, this would eliminate it.

I knew the one thing the Indians appreciated was respect. Showing some might just save us. I ordered the boys to each grab an arm as I took hold of the man's legs. Together, we nervously carried the body another twenty yards into the desert away from our wagons. I positioned the brave laying on his back, with his legs lying straight and his arms folded across his chest. Not wasting any time, we hurried back to the safety of our camp.

"Seth, go down to the other end and get a couple of men to help you do just as we did here. I'm betting you'll be safe, just as we were out there. Let's hope a show of respect might help us survive the night. It could be the single factor to keep them from sending another attack. But be careful. I don't want to lose you, or anyone else." Turning my head to Jess, I continued, "Jess, get my horse ready for me. You two had it easy, sittin' on your butts in the wagon. I'm worn out running from one end of camp to the other. After you get that done, check and see how many dead and injured we have. Also, inform all the guards to aim for their heads if we're attacked again. It seems to be the only place our bullets have any effect. There's a lot of scared people right now. It's our job to make sure they're calmed down and ready to leave at daybreak. I don't want to stay here any longer than we have to."

Leaning against a wagon wheel, I rested as the two headed off to do as asked. They were good men. I hadn't heard a thing about Jess doing any woman chasing this trip and Seth seemed to have returned to his old self. Both were ready to be wagon masters. Yet, I wondered if this experience might change their thoughts of becoming one in the future. I hoped not. They'd have no trouble earning respect and trust as a wagon master. Hell, I trusted both with my life. It was a trust they had earned.

"Well, that was interesting."

"Spoonman, where in the hell were you?" I knew he had been in the fray, but where he had fought from was a mystery. "Don't tell me you were hiding under a box or two of supplies."

"Hiding? Me? You dumb son-of-a-bitch, you know better," he cussed, knowing I was giving him a hard time. "I was in the wagon with your woman and son-to-be. That's where I was. I figured if you weren't going to protect them, I might as well. I've got used to them helping me out. You made me too lazy to do all the cooking and cleaning up by myself. I need 'em, even if you don't! By the way, it was my bullet that blew apart the skull of the creature first. Jess and Seth couldn't hit the damn side of the plateau behind us if they were ten feet away from it!"

"You better check to make sure they didn't throw out all your damn beans while you were playing games," I retorted, a smile crossing my face for the first time in hours. "I'd hate to have to fill your wagon with rattlesnakes to supply us with something to eat the rest of the trip."

"You ain't got to eat 'em. Go find yourself some peyote to munch on and go crazy, you damn fool. Bet it wouldn't do anything to you … you're already crazy!" Grumbling, Spoonman spun around and climbed up in his wagon. The old guy didn't know how much I loved having him around. Or, maybe he did. We had grown accustomed to each other over the years.

"You love giving him a hard time, don't you?"

"If you had been an Indian, I would be dead right now," I whispered to the woman who had silently come up beside me. "What did you do, climb out of the other end of your wagon so you could sneak up on me?"

"I have to admit, I was eavesdropping on you and Spoonman," Sarah whispered, as if she'd performed the ultimate sin. "He called me your woman and Kincaid your son-to-be. Does he know something you and I don't?"

"When you've known Spoonman as long as I have, you'll know to believe about half of what he says, and forget the other half," I responded, wishing the old man had kept his tongue from wagging. I didn't need him playing matchmaker, not now. "We need to make it to the end of our journey before any of us make plans. After tonight's attack by these creatures, I don't know if any of us have much of a future."

Leaning forward, Sarah took hold of my hands and gazed into my eyes. "Well, I'm not one for waiting." With that, she stood up on her tip toes and placed her lips on mine.

Gradually, she placed her arms around me and pulled me close. I must admit, having her body against mine brought out feelings I hadn't felt in years. I wanted to pull her tight and take her, right then and there, but I kept my arms at my sides. Finishing her extended kiss, she leaned back a few inches and whispered with her hot breath, "Do you want more?"

Taking her arms from around my waist, I gently placed them along her sides. "I do, but let's hold off until the end of the trip. Then, we won't have to worry about interruptions … or reputations."

"What a fucking coward!" Spoonman's rasps echoed from behind his wagon canvas. His guff-haws and laughter made Sarah and I smile. About that time, another chuckled behind us. Jess had just arrived with my horse and had also overheard our special moment.

Like I had said … interruptions.

Chapter Seven

"Hard to believe two Indians killed twelve people and injured seven others, isn't it?"

We had been moving a couple of hours, having left our campsite at daybreak. The final tally was in and, sadly, all those killed or injured were husbands and fathers. Three wagons had been destroyed by fire, as well. Many dreams of a new life had drastically changed overnight.

"You know they weren't just Indian warriors," I replied to Seth, riding beside me. "And, only one of them actually killed the twelve. You guys got the other before he could get to us and do any damage. The rules of the game have been rewritten. Where we thought ourselves prepared, all of a sudden, we're fighting monsters. With the change in enemy, I don't want to jeopardize losing you or Jess by sending you ahead to scout out the trail. You might end up like the guides did. So, we're traveling blind right now. We'll have to deal with whatever is ahead when we come to it."

"I heard Ternam got injured by one of those creatures last night," Seth continued, knowing my dislike of the man. "Supposedly, he had gone out to save a child and got smashed on the back of the head. Kind of makes him a hero, doesn't it?"

I pulled back hard on my reins, stopping my horse. "He's saying what? That bastard was using the child as a shield against imaginary arrows or as a sacrificial offering, so I rammed the butt of my Winchester against his damn skull!"

"All I know is that's what he's telling folks. Maybe you need to set things straight."

Enough was enough, especially when it came to cowards. I whipped my horse around, ordered Spoonman to stop his team and the wagon train, and headed back for a confrontation with Mr. Ternam.

Sighting his wagon, I prepared myself for what I needed to do. My first thoughts were to send him and his family out to survive on their own. If the man hadn't had three children, I probably would have, but I couldn't make his kids suffer for his cowardice. No, the man needed to be embarrassed … embarrassed so bad he would never live it down. I wanted the title of "Coward" to be branded into his forehead, for all to see.

Pulling up to his wagon, I was shocked at the sight of his wife driving the team of horses. Sitting beside her was her "poor and brave" husband, his head wrapped with a huge bandage. "Ternam, get down off your wagon. I'm calling you out here and now, in front of everyone to see. Get down now or I swear I'll come up there and throw you off the wagon myself."

"You going to congratulate him for saving the child?" came a voice from the wagon in front of his.

"No, I'm calling him out for being a lying coward!" I shouted back, not holding my anger inside.

"Now, now, I've been injured by one of those beasts that attacked us last night," he murmured, acting as if he deserved sympathy, instead of castigation. "I'm afraid if I get down, I'll pass out."

"Well, let's see if that happens," I growled as I climbed off my horse and shot up the wagon's steps to where he sat. Grabbing his shoulders, I lifted him up and used all my strength to throw the bastard off and to the ground. As he tried to crawl away, I kicked him in his ribs several times, before ending my attack with a kick to his butt. Rolling over onto his back, Ternam begged for mercy. Several men from nearby wagons rushed to his assistance. Facing them, I pulled my pistol, shot once into the air, and pointed it at the crowd until they backed away.

"Your damn hero is a lying coward, just like I said," I hollered out, knowing this was the time to make Ternam squirm. "I was running to help those in one of the burning wagons last night and caught him holding a child out to the darkness in front of him. I don't know if he had seen the creatures and wanted to offer her in hopes it would leave him alone, or if he thought the Indians would be shooting arrows into the camp and figured it was better for her to get one in the heart than him. I smashed my damn Winchester against his head, so he'd let her go. I should've shot the bastard."

"No, that's not what happened," Ternam whined out, still on his back in the dirt. "I was saving the child."

"That's exactly what happened," a woman's voice sounded out from the crowd. "It was my daughter he took. I tried to fight him, but he knocked me away. All I could do was try to save my other children. Then, Grant saved my daughter by knocking Terman down to the ground. I kept quiet earlier, when Ternam lied about what happened, because I didn't think anyone would believe me."

You could have heard a pin drop on the desert sand. Only the sound of Ternam's sobbing over being called out for the coward he was remained. There he lay, his hands over his eyes, expressing his innocence and proclaiming all others as liars. He was a pitiful sight.

Disgusted at how they'd fallen for his tale of heroism, the crowd broke up and went back to their wagons. I glanced up at Ternam's wife and kids looking down at

him and the tears rolling down their cheeks. I felt sorry
for them and hated they be penalized for his actions any
further, but I had to take a stance. "Ternam, you and
your wagon wait until all the others pass. You take the
rear and eat everyone's dust. No one should have to
smell your cowardly stink by having to follow you. For
the rest of the journey you stay there, keep your mouth
shut, and don't ever bother another person here. If you
do, you're out on your own. That's a promise!"

I mounted up and rode back to the head of the wagon
train, giving Spoonman the order to start moving again.
After a few minutes, I sent Seth back to make sure
Ternam was in the rear. Not saying I didn't trust him,
but I didn't trust him.

By mid-afternoon, we had reached the part of the trail
I dreaded most. For the next couple of days or so, we
would be most vulnerable to attack. Our route would
have us on a narrow passage, sometimes only wide
enough for a single wagon, with a cliff wall to the north
side and a deep ravine to the south. Not only would we
have to deal with the usual trail hazards of a team getting
spooked and dropping over the edge, but there was the
possibility of our enemies launching a full-scale attack
from atop the cliff wall. I suspected they might even
start a landslide before we made it through. What scared
me most was we would be forced to camp overnight in a

single file line, only inches from the ravine's lip. There was little to no margin for error.

"Let's hold up here for the night and get started again in the morning," I suggested to the boys, both nodding, happy to oblige. Kneeling, I drew out my wagon arrangement for the night's camp in the sand. "Tonight, let's arrange the wagons differently. I want four circles with twenty wagons each. If we put them in a box formation, each circle will have two sides against other wagons. Once those are in position, take the rest of the wagons and box in the four circles already in place. All our guard watches will be in this outer ring of wagons. The womenfolk, children, livestock, and those too injured to do anything will stay inside their own areas. At minimum, this will give us double-wall protection for them, as well as keep the guards from having to worry about a rear attack."

"Damn, Boss," Seth exhaled, wiping his forehead with his forearm. "How long did it take you to come up with that? You sure know how to complicate things, don't you?"

"Would you rather work harder and be safe, or have it easy and be dead in the morning?" I answered in a monotone. I had predicted one of the two would say something about my plan, so I'd prepared myself in advance. "As much as we all hate Spoonman's beans, I

91

believe they're better than never eating anything again, don't you?"

Both nodded and remained solemn. I'd wasted a joke on them. Maybe I had used it too many times.

"One thing about your plan I don't like, Boss," Jess spoke out, surprising Seth and me. "If we find we need to break camp and run because of their numbers, it's going to be impossible to do."

"I don't see running an option like it has been in the past," I replied in a steady tone. This was the first time Jess had ever challenged me in any way. I kind of liked it … as long as it didn't become a habit. "Breakaways only work if you've got a small wagon train and somewhere to go. We're too damn big and the only place we could run to would be the passage. That's not the place to be running. Plus, they'd get more than half the wagons if we tried. And, if they use those creatures on us again, they're faster than any wagon team, even at full speed. We'd only be signing death warrants for most of those who trust us. This is a "stand or die" situation. I'm hoping all these inner walls will give enough cover to protect us better than ever before."

Nodding his silent agreement, he and Seth set out to do as told. An hour later, amidst a wave of profanity and negative comments from those driving the wagons, the camp was set up and ready for the night. With Ternam's wagon the last to be moved into position, I'd arranged for it to be directly in front of the pass leading through the canyons. It would serve him well to have every wagon pass him the next morning as he waited to take his place as last in line.

Groups gathered up dried brush and any scattered wood lying around to start the camp's fires, and the routine of clearing the area of rattlesnakes brought in a few for the evening skillets. The watch was set and checked to ensure maximum security way before any hit the hay for the night. I wanted us to be ready should a repeat of the previous night await.

After forcing down a plate of beans (Sarah's tasting almost as bad to me now as Spoonman's), I lay back under Spoonman's wagon to catch a quick nap. Seth's watch would be over in a few hours and I would relieve him. Jess's turn would follow me, around three in the morning. His snores, and Spoonman's from inside the wagon, didn't help me have much success in getting rest. Add in worries of a night attack, and passing fancies of a future life with Sarah, and one might say I got more sleep on my horse during the day than under my blanket that night.

I had almost made it to dreamland when Seth shook me to relieve him. After checking my boots for scorpions and snakes before putting them on, and

93

making sure my rifle and pistol were ready for action, I rolled up my blanket and trudged out from under the wagon. It felt good to leave the sound of Spoonman's snoring behind. Quickly, I challenged the chill of the desert's night air with a hot cup of coffee and the warmth of a dwindling fire. To get the flames roaring again, I tossed in a busted-up plank from one of the wagons of the previous night's victims. I was pleased I had thought to have the men bust them apart and collect their wood before we had left that morning. There was plenty of brush to use in the desert, but it burned up fast and made tending the fire a constant chore. The long-burning wood from the wagons was better served to keep the fires going than rotting away by the graves of their past owners.

Finishing my coffee, I listened as Seth filled me in on the evening so far. Things had been quiet, for the most part. He didn't have to tell me how scared folks were, but did so anyway. I figured things would be tense after last night. Folks were worried about what they'd faced and feared the chances of having to do it again. I had known they'd either pull together or start jumping down each other's throats. It was good to see them realize depending on each other was the only way we'd get out of this mess. None on watch had been caught sleeping, which was a surprise. Most had gotten little to no sleep in the last twenty-four hours.

I let Seth finish, told him to get some sleep, and began my watch. Walking about, the sound of hammers cocking at my presence was a sign all were awake, but also one to be wary of hearing. Folks have been killed too many times by accident, or incidents called accidents to escape prosecution.

"So, do you think they'll attack again tonight?"

I was a little surprised to hear a woman's voice up and about this time of night. Turning, I saw Mrs. Ternam dropping a plank on the fire by her wagon. The sparks shot up as if they wanted to get closer to the moon above and see if the man there was really smiling down upon them. "I'm hoping they don't, but it's better to be ready if they do."

"I'm hoping they don't, as well, like everyone else here," she stammered, placing a coffee pot close to the fire. "I tried sleeping but didn't have much luck. I can't forget about last night's attack. Figured I'd make some coffee for those on watch. My husband was just relieved of his shift and passed out as soon as he laid down. Nothing bothers him, not even the fact no one will talk to us now. Watch him, Wagon Master, watch him. He's a vengeful man."

"I appreciate the warning, Mrs. Ternam," I spoke out, keeping my voice low. "I don't think being his friend was ever a priority with me. From what I can see, he's a bully and a liar, who isn't happy unless he has his own way. I hate that you and the children must suffer for his being that way. You seem to be a nice lady."

"Oh, I'm used to it," she sighed, shaking her head as if she'd been through it before. "A wife is always stuck walking in her husband's footprints, whether she wants to or not. His mouth got us in trouble back in Tennessee. He was always telling his employers how they needed to run things and trying to take control from them. Never could keep a job. Sometimes we ate, sometimes we didn't … kind of like now. He seemed to think coming out West would be a chance for him to have his own property and run it the way he wanted. Me and the kids didn't have much choice but to come with him. It was either that … or start begging."

I let her pour some fresh coffee in my tin cup and thanked her, before moving on. There wasn't anything I could do to make her plight any easier. Like many women, I guessed she had probably been pushed by her parents into marriage at fourteen or fifteen, and had resolved herself to be the man's wife, regardless of how he acted. Of course, after the children had entered the picture, her chances of leaving him had been totally erased, if they had ever existed. Shame she was stuck with him.

I began to wonder how many of the other women weren't happy with the men they'd chosen to live with the rest of their lives. I'd heard of men killing their wives if they were unhappy, and getting away with it by saying they'd run off with another man. People actually felt sorry for them. Yet, women seemed to be stuck with their man until he either died or was killed. Didn't seem fair.

As I continued my rounds, most of the men on guard were wide awake and alert. I had only caught one almost snoozing. When told of the reason, I understood. He had just gotten off watch the night before when we were attacked. Though tired, he had helped the others after the battle bury the dead. Tonight, while skinning one of the rattlers he had caught for dinner, his toddler son had found one of the heads he had just cut off and picked it up. By reflex, its fangs had sunk their venom into the boy's tiny hand. The father had ignored getting any sleep as he and his wife had been up all night with the boy, doing their best to keep the swelling down, without success. Now, exhausted, his staying awake on guard had become an impossibility.

If I had known this, he wouldn't have been placed in watch rotation. I took his position for a couple of hours to let the man sleep until his relief showed up. Then, together, we went to check on his son. I had to hold back my tears when his wife clutched hold of her husband and told him the boy had died. No child should die before their parents. It's a sorrow none should have to bear.

I was heavy with the sadness of being reminded death was our constant companion out on the trail as I returned to the wagon. The Grim Reaper didn't discriminate when he dropped in … all were fair game. After waking up and briefing Jess, I covered up under my blanket and lay back. Life was filled with hardships. People not meant for each other being forced to live together, children not being able to see their adult years, and even folks living in fear of being killed by monsters … none of it made any sense. If God was kind and loving, how could he make people suffer in such manners? Surely, he would have more mercy on the deserving good folks and let the devil take care of the bad … wouldn't he?

Oh, I'd heard the preachers shouting out their promises of our reward in Heaven coming after death. "You gotta suffer down here on Earth so ye can reap the golden benefits of God's love when your spirit is given entrance through the wondrous gates of Heaven," they had all shouted out, in one way or another. Yet, if all we knew life on Earth was the bad part, how could we be sure the preachers weren't evil, as well, and lying to us about what comes when we die?

Now, I'm not saying I don't believe in God, because I do. If you believe in the Devil, which anyone who had seen the creatures the night before would have to, then you'd have to believe in God. After last night, we were all praying our asses off to him for mercy and protection. It just seemed that the Devil didn't take as many days off as God did. Seemed like something bad was always happening, and the good occurrences were somewhat sparse, especially on a wagon train.

Yet, Sarah had entered my life. Deciding if that was a good or bad thing would have to wait until later.

Chapter Eight

"If you're a wanting any breakfast, you better get your lazy butt up. I ain't got all day to wait on you. There's chores to be done and wagons a waitin' to move on!"

When I was a child, there were times my parents would let me visit my grandparents and spend a week or so with them. I remember being roused from a sound sleep by an old rooster crowing at daybreak each morning. Oh, how I hated that rooster. These days, I can't get over how I would prefer the sound of that damn rooster to Spoonman's raspy voice.

"Don't want nothing to eat," I mumbled out, trying to keep my stomach safe from another plate of beans. "Go ahead and clean up and get ready to move out. I'll be up and about shortly."

"Damn, I been waitin' and waitin'," the sound of his grumbling faded as he stormed off. "Can't believe how lazy some people get when they get old. Don't even want to use the energy to get up and eat."

Thirty minutes later, we were on our way to the rugged pass through the canyon. I had divided the train up into thirds, with me taking the lead position, Seth in the second spot, and Jess responsible for the last group. Progress was going to be slow, but care and concentration were going to be required, both in driving the teams, and in keeping an eye out for a possible attack.

The Indians had taken it easy on us the night before, by allowing us a night of peace. I figured they did so for two reasons. The first was obvious. There was no reason to hurry. The trail ahead would give them plenty of opportunity to attack and sustain minimal losses. The second was the one that scared me the most. The hell with what the government thought about the "dumb and uncivilized" red man … Indians are smart. In fact, they're a lot smarter than most of those in Washington. I believed they wanted our people to gain a false sense of security, you know, think they were safe, so we'd relax our guard. That would make their attacks not only safer for them, but easier and much more effective.

It didn't take us long to get our first glimpse of the ravine. One wrong move and you'd have plenty of time to think about your mistake before ever reaching bottom. I let the boys in on it, but Spoonman knew I was nervous about this part of our journey for another reason. I didn't like being in high places. As a child, I used to climb a lot of trees. One afternoon, I was pushing my luck and inched out too far on a limb. It gave way and I went tumbling, my fall only being slowed by my smacking into lower limbs and scrambling to grab hold of any branch I could. I hit the ground hard and broke one of my legs. The doctor made me stay in bed the rest of the summer and most of the fall months. Ever since, high places reminded me of that experience.

I'd made the mistake of telling Spoonman my story a few trips back, during a trip through a mountain pass like this one, only further south. For miles, he had taunted me, "Careful, don't look down" and "Oops, there you go ... down further and further and further ... damn, you're almost to the bottom ... look out!" I was so mad I had almost fired him, once we'd made it through the pass.

It was slow going for most of the day. The sound of whips lashing out as the teams struggled to pull their loads and shouts of "Move it on" had echoed throughout the canyon. We had stopped several times for a few minutes, to give the wagon teams a rest. The steep incline had already taken quite a toll on the animals. I figured, at the rate we were going, we should hit the highest point by late afternoon. We would be halfway through, with the easiest part of the trail waiting to be conquered the next day. But it was the night ahead that bothered me. With all the noise we had made, I was sure if there were any Indians around, they would know exactly where we were.

Without warning, my horse reared up on his hind legs and nearly threw me off. Fighting to gain control of him, I yanked hard on the reins trying to move him to the wall. Refusing to abide my commands, he backed away and inched toward the edge of the ravine. Over my shoulder, I could see the river far below, no wider than a thin ribbon, with dots where boulders lay along its banks. Fighting my fear of heights, I dug my heels hard into my horse's ribcage, doing my best to get him to move forward and away from the edge. Snorting and huffing, he finally turned toward Spoonman's wagon and trotted to the horse team.

A little relieved at his changing his mind about committing suicide, my peace of mind was short-lived as I watched Spoonman stand tall and raise his rifle. *What the hell are you doing? Surely, you're not aiming at me. Are we being attacked from ahead?* I spun my head around as he fired, just in time to see what had spooked my horse so bad. The body of a huge rattler fell from atop a high rock and started twisting and flopping on the trail, its reflexes keeping it moving about for several minutes. Climbing down from his wagon, he trod up to the snake and used the barrel of his rifle to flip it over the edge.

"Damn, why'd I do that. It could've been supper. Hey, Grant, need to change your pants?" Spoonman roared out, laughing only as Spoonman could do. "I got a spare pair in the wagon, if you do. Don't want the ones you crapped in, though. You keep them with you or throw them down in the river if you get close enough to the edge. Bad enough I'd have to smell them with you being so close, but I damn sure don't want them in the wagon!"

"Take five minutes and rest the animals," I hollered back, embarrassed by his comments. "When we start up again, I'll be walking to make sure we don't have a repeat performance. And, if I had messed my pants, I'd be smearing them in your face to shut that damn mouth of yours, old man!"

"Old man? Who you calling, 'Old Man?'" Spoonman's ire had been raised and I loved it. "You ain't much younger than me, not nearly as smart, and your eyes are going bad. You didn't even see that rattler."

I had known being the only one in front of the train would put me at risk and the episode with the deadly reptile had reminded me that hostiles were not the only thing we needed to watch for. Taking the lead role, I was going to be the first one to meet any further snakes or other wild animals, as well as be the first to feel bullets or arrows entering my flesh from any hostiles. Choosing not to risk sending out any advance scouts had been a bad decision, but it was too late to do anything about it.

The trail had become so narrow, there was no way to squeeze a horse and rider by any of the wagons. We were a row of ducks all lined up, waiting to become a wolf's meal, and I would be the first course.

Wrapping the reins around my fingers, we started forward once again with me leading my horse. After a few miles, the sun's scorching rays had heated up the rock wall beside us to almost a melting point. Soon, the sweltering temperature had me soaked in sweat and my throat begging for a drink of water. I could only imagine how bad it had to be on the horse and oxen teams pulling the wagons. Progress became even slower than expected. Still, we pushed on until the trail finally leveled off just before dusk. After another half an hour, when notified the last wagon, Ternam's, had finally reached the level area, we stopped for the night.

"Make sure everyone knows there will be no fires tonight. Also, everyone sleeps under their wagons," I relayed to Spoonman as I thought us most vulnerable from attack above. "No exceptions. If we're attacked from above, we don't need any fires giving the Indians clear targets to aim at. Also, the wagon bottoms will stop a lot of arrows that the canvas alone won't. I hope you weren't expecting a lot of sleep, as I don't expect any of us to get much. If it wasn't too dangerous to keep going in the dark, we would. I don't like this spot at all."

"You think they're above us, don't you?" he asked, his frown showing his concern. "I do, too. I got a feeling. They are above us right now, just waiting for the right moment to attack."

We went hungry for the night. I figured if we were still alive the next day, we'd eat then. I just didn't want the light or smoke from the fires drawing attention. Exhausted and ready to pass out, I pulled Spoonman aside. "Keep your eyes open and rifle ready for an hour or two. I gotta get a couple of hours of sleep. All that walking wore me out. When you wake me, I'll go up the trail fifty yards or so and stand watch. Hopefully, if any of them come at us from the west, I can stop at least one or two of them. My rifle shots will tell you there's an attack coming. If you see any heading this way, I'm probably dead. Don't worry about your bullets hitting me. Shoot like hell and shoot to kill."

Three hours later, I was leaning against the side of the cliff wall and doing my best to remain unseen. The full moon had taken its place in the sky and was doing its best to lighten the night enough to expose my position to anyone coming up the trail. Around two o'clock in the morning, the first flaming arrow was shot from atop the cliff wall. By chance, I had turned to see if all was well behind me when it soared from its bow and landed on a wagon below. One of the men on watch had seen it, as well, pulled it from the wagon, and sent it into the ravine before it could do much damage. Other arrows followed and multiple shots rang out from the rear of the train. There was no doubt. This was the attack I had feared. This night, men and women would die.

As barrage after barrage of arrows landed, the flames from the burning wagons panicked the livestock. With nowhere else to go, many fell over the ravine's edge to their deaths. With the cliff walls being so high and steep, our people found the targets above at an impossible angle to get in their rifle sights. Helpless, they could do little but hide under their wagons until the rain of arrows ceased. Many of those who refused to take cover were dying as they did their best to remove the burning canvas from atop their wagons. Those wagons, too far gone to save, were sent over the edge, landing on some of the dead livestock who had reached the bottom before them. Soon, the acrid smell of burning animal hide and flesh filled the canyon.

I will never forget the screams of the injured and dying. It haunts me to this day.

There was nothing I could do.

I had stayed at my position, about fifty yards in front of the train. There was a slight break in the cliff wall I had come upon and used to conceal myself while watching the trail ahead. I'd been lucky, so far, and been undiscovered by those above. The train had been attacked from the rear and above. I was sure the next would come from my direction.

As those behind me battled to control animals and fires, I kept close watch. Within minutes, three braves, keeping to the shadows as best they could, came into view. I was almost to the point of squeezing the trigger on my Winchester when they halted and began to shed their clothing. Once naked, they extended their arms toward the moon and began to chant, as if hoping their gods would hear them. Within seconds, their chants began sounding more like groans of pain.

The best I could tell under the dim light of the night sky, these were average sized men. Yet, the more they stretched up and out toward the heavens, the taller and broader they got. Fingers lengthened and hooked claws grew from their fingertips. Their heads began to transform, all facial features extending and changing into what looked like snouts, resembling those of wolves. Thick fur began to cover their bodies and their groans became snarls.

I had to act.

My first shot shattered the head of the closest. Falling back, the second, eyes reflecting the flames behind me, caught sight of my position, and leapt toward me. Taking aim, I fired twice more. He, too, joined his fellow brave on the canyon trail … dead. The third, now fully transformed, rushed forward. I chambered my final cartridge and pulled the trigger.

Somehow, I missed, the bullet whizzing past him. He was too close to reload. I pulled my pistol and fired, my last shot exploding in the face of the beast as its claws sliced down my left arm. I fought to hold on to my gun and fired again and again, until it was empty. Blinded, the beast backed away, and stumbled to the edge of the ravine while clawing at the air, hoping to block any other bullets heading its way. Mortally wounded, it spun around in pain to find only emptiness under its feet. A mournful howl penetrated the night as it fell to its death.

My arm gushing blood, I ripped off my jacket and did my best to wrap it tightly around my wounds. I reloaded both my rifle and pistol and lay back down against the cliff wall. I was groggy from the loss of blood and could feel my consciousness slowly departing. Fighting to stay awake, I tried to concentrate on my wounds and the agony they were bringing me. From behind me, shots continued to ring out. The battle wasn't over. I needed to stay awake and be a part of it. I had to keep my eyes peeled for any more braves, human or monster, who might try to get by me and enter the fray.

The pounding in my head was like that of Indian drums. Over and over, the beat repeated itself. I saw a vision of more beasts dancing around a huge bonfire, hypnotized by the rhythm and working themselves into a frenzy to attack any and all who faced off against them. They had the advantage. They were the strong. They would know no defeat.

Smoke from their bonfire in my mind burned my eyes. A cloud drifted between the flames and me. My vision faded away and darkness eliminated my ability to see. I passed out.

Chapter Nine

"… and, now that you're awake, I need to let you know the facts."

The voice above me was as out of focus as the face it came from. I could tell it was Seth's, but it sounded much different. It was the voice of one who had been through hell, one who had seen terrible things and hated talking about them. This was no longer the voice of a young man. This was the voice of a man in charge.

"We have about seventy wagons left after last night's attack," he continued, thinking I was fully able to comprehend what he was saying. I wanted to shout out for him to wait a few minutes until I entered that level of consciousness, but hesitated, knowing he had higher priorities to manage. "There are sixty-four dead, including Jess, and seventy-three with some sort of injury. We've salvaged all the supplies and ammunition out of the wagons of the dead that hadn't burned up or already been shoved off into the ravine. The men busted up and salvaged what they could for tonight's camp firewood. Everything else that no one wanted was sent over the edge into the ravine."

Seth took a breath and steadied himself. It wasn't hard to see he had seen more death and destruction in a few hours than he had ever witnessed before. "I've got enough people, some uninjured and some with minor wounds or burns, to handle the remaining wagons and get us moving again. The trip down will be faster than the trip up was, I hope. We should hit flat land again late this afternoon if we start now. There's no time to waste. I'll take the lead and you stay here. You're in no condition to do anything but lay on your back right now. You lost too much blood and are as pale as a ghost. I imagine you're pretty damn weak. Don't worry, I've got this. You rest."

At that moment, I couldn't do anything else but nod.

"He's done a good job this morning," Spoonman muttered, preparing himself to take the reins of his team in a few minutes. "Carried you back here by himself, he did, no one helped him. Told me he'd kill me if I let you die. Sounded a lot like you did when you were a younger man. You trained him right."

Again, I nodded, not sure of being able to speak, or even wanting to try. So, Jess was dead and Seth was in command. Seth could handle it. Jess could have as well, if he had survived. I wanted to know how he had died but asked myself, "Does it matter? He's dead." Still, I yearned to hear the details of the attack. Had the beasts attacked the rear first, or had the shooting been at normal braves. How much of the livestock had survived? Had any children been killed? Too many questions. Too many details. Too many had died in the attack and there would probably be some of the injured to join them before we got to the bottom. My heart was heavy.

I tried to move my left arm and immediately regretted it. Although wrapped from top to bottom in bandages, I could feel the strain of my effort pull against the stitches someone had sewn to hold my flesh together. It would be a while before I'd be able to use it normally … if ever.

A hard jerk, as Spoonman got the horses moving, shot the pain from my arm up through my neck. I'd had knife wounds that didn't hurt so bad and wondered if some sort of poison might have been used to paint the claws of the beasts to make them more lethal. I could tell this was one trip I wasn't going to enjoy. Every time the wagon fought to roll over a good-sized rock, I was jostled about. The wagon's speed increased as the descent from the top made the going much easier on the horses, but much harder on me enduring the agony of my wounds. With each bump, a lightning bolt of pain flashed by my eyes and tried to exit out the top of my skull. I was miserable.

I dozed from time to time, but there was no peace in sleep. Nightmares of those insidious wolf-like creatures—their huge bodies covered with black matted fur, the sound of their evil snarling, the reflection of fire in their eyes, and their canine incisors dripping with the blood of their victims—never ceased. No matter which way I turned, there was always one in front of me, rushing forward with a desire to rip the flesh from my bones and savor the taste of my still-beating heart in its mouth.

Yet, just before my flesh felt them tear into my body, I would awaken, my clothes drenched in cold sweat, my body chilled and shivering, and my wounds throbbing. I wanted to scream out, "Stop the wagons!" I stayed silent, gritting my teeth and tightening up every muscle in my body, in an attempt to hold myself together. I wasn't a child, but an adult, one in control. The wagon train's safety depended on advancing down the mountain as fast as caution would allow. Our numbers, decreasing ever so fast, were working in the favor of the Indians and their chances of entirely wiping us out.

I had never been one to surrender, but I had to wonder how could we think of surviving if they ever decided to send all those able to transform at once? The thought of us facing such a swarm was ludicrous. I could only imagine them darting from victim to victim, destroying lives and futures of those who had only wanted to better their existence. Yes, we would lose the battle and the beasts would gather to howl at the moon amid the carnage as our dismembered bodies soaked the desert floor with blood.

We needed a plan to keep that from happening. It was my responsibility to come up with one.

I woke to voices outside the wagon. "He's been sleeping all day" ... "The fever's got him" ... "He must be fighting every monster in his dreams" ... Spoonman and Seth talking as if I wasn't going to make it. Yet, death wasn't an option. I had to keep going. I was the Wagon Master, not Seth, and I'd be damned if I didn't make every attempt possible to keep my promise of getting these people to their destination alive.

"You can stop talking about me and start talking to me, if you two aren't too damn busy," I spoke out, using what little energy I could scrape up to make myself heard. The wagon tilted under the weight of the two as they hurried to get to me, sending another jolt up my arm. I could see the concern on their faces as they opened the canvas. "From the looks I'm getting from you two, I'm already dead. Personally, I think I must be doing pretty damn good if you two haven't decided to bury me, yet."

"You're too damn ornery to die," Spoonman whispered, as if he understood speaking in a loud voice would cause my head to explode. "I was wonderin' if you were ever going to wake up. Nothin' like being lazy and shirking your duties."

Same old Spoonman, not one to give me a break, even when wounded. I hoped he never changed.

"Hey, Boss, I got so much to tell you, but there's so little time," Seth blurted out, the pressure of command obviously getting to him. "I got the wagons set for the night. I think we'll be safe, but after last night, nothing's for sure. We lost six more people today. Four of them were injured last night in the attack, and two got a wagon too close to the ravine's edge and went over the side. No chance of them being alive after such a fall. We left them at the bottom of the ravine. I need to get the watch list up for tonight, although I don't have much to work with. Too many injured and hurting, like yourself. But, don't worry, I'll handle it. You just lay back and rest up. I want you back in charge as soon as possible."

I acknowledged Seth's report and gave him and Spoonman additional instructions on what needed to be done before anything else. Seth nodded his understanding and immediately set out to see it completed. I had to give it to the man, he was having to handle it all with depleted resources and little help from anyone. It was his trial by fire. I just hoped we all didn't get burned in the process.

"In case you might be curious, your woman and her son made it through the attack last night. The boy did good. Got himself one of those creatures you let get by. Shot him right between the eyes."

Spoonman's news couldn't have come at a better time. That was one worry I could relieve myself of, one that should never have been present at all. In my nightmares, I'd seen their bodies torn apart and eaten by the wild beasts. I had feared to ask if that had been the case.

Refusing to lay back down, I had Spoonman help me out of the wagon and to the ground. Sitting with my back against a wagon wheel, I scanned over the camp. Seth had done a good job in setting up the wagons in a double circle formation. The manpower problem he was having in finding enough guards was painfully evident, as the walking wounded were everywhere. Yet, where the men were scattered about, their wives and older children were substituting in their places. Noticing even the wounded were armed, I had Spoonman bring me my weapons. My arm felt as if it had swollen to twice its normal size and was stiff as a board. Raising my Winchester up to shoot might be a problem, but I could still handle my pistol if the need arose.

"I know you don't want these, but eat them anyway. You need to get something in your body to build up your strength." Spoonman set a plate of beans down in my lap and a cup of coffee on the ground to my side. As he walked away, his being nice ended quickly, as always. "And don't let me hear you bitchin' about my beans. You're lucky to be alive to eat them."

Surprisingly, I ate every one of them. They almost tasted good … almost.

Sitting there while sipping my coffee, I couldn't shake the feeling we weren't out of the woods, yet. The Indians had made good on their promises so far, and I didn't expect them to quit now. Last night's attack had hurt us bad. But, as dangerous as it had been, if the trail hadn't been so narrow, it could have been worse. In talking to Spoonman, I learned the men in the rear of the train had set up two ranks, who shot the attacking beasts in volleys. It was an old technique utilized by the British Army during the Revolutionary War that had failed them in open combat, but had worked well within the restrictions of the narrow trail. By all counts, only four had attacked us from the front, and ten from the rear. Each had been killed without one of us feeling their savagery, besides my wounds, that is. All our dead and injured had come from the arrow barrages, including Jess, who had been playing the hero and helping others find cover first.

I wished I had taught him none of us are invincible.

As usual, I could only shake my head when he told me of the actions of my favorite traveler, Mr. Ternam. As the others were setting up their ranks behind his wagon, he had gathered his family and fled closer to the middle of the wagon train. Finding the widow and children of one killed in the first night's attack, he had forced them out from beneath their wagon and positioned his family in their place. The widow and her two young girls had been killed, but Ternam and his family were untouched.

"I swear, if the Indians, monsters, or you don't kill that man, I'm going to," Spoonman spit out as he stood up, hands on his hips, and searched out the man's location. "I ain't never hated a man so much as him. Damn coward, he is. Not worth piss in the pot."

I agreed. To imagine anyone standing up for the man after all the things he had done was inconceivable. Exposed for being a coward, the man did nothing to demonstrate otherwise and continued to play the role well. If I had been well enough, I would've answered Spoonman's request.

"Why don't we move you under the wagon so you can lay down and get some sleep?"

I turned my head to find Sarah kneeling beside me. "You have a habit of sneaking up on me. Are you sure you're not part Indian?"

Spoonman chuckled as he walked away.

"I need to check your wounds first, though," she whispered, continuing to act as if she were responsible for me. "You had some deep slashes I had to sew up last night. I'm hoping the stitches didn't rip free from all the bouncing around in the wagon, today."

"So, you were the one that sewed me up," I exclaimed, a little shocked at this new revelation. "All this time I was blaming Spoonman for the pain I was in. I almost feel guilty."

"You can blame me, if you wish," she whispered, a smile appearing on her face. "You can blame me all the way to California, and long after, if you want. As long as you include me in your life in some way, you can blame me forever and I'll be happy."

For a moment, I had the strongest urge to lean forward and kiss her. Then, when she started removing the bandages, the pain made me want to kill her. Yeah, I was in love.

Sarah had just finished cleaning my wounds and reapplying the bandages when the first shots rang out.

"First group, fire only when you can be sure you'll hit them in the head. Second group, wait until the first shot hits, then fire!"

It was still early, but we were under attack! Seth's commands were loud and clear. He had once more set up a planned volley attack on those charging our position. Knowing many of the women and children had never been forced to shoot while being attacked, he was going to control their ammunition usage by ordering them when to shoot. It was an admirable plan. One I probably wouldn't have considered. I just hoped it worked!

Sarah gave me a quick peck on the cheek and hurried off to take her place next to her son. She was one of the soldiers now, one who would protect those unable to protect themselves. I rolled to my stomach and rested my Winchester's barrel upon a wagon wheel spoke. Pointing it at a huge figure rushing my way, I did my best to aim, and fired. I almost cheered as the bullet hit the creature and sent it to its backside. As it tried to rise, another one of my shots sent it down permanently. But, before I could take a breath, another creature took its place and headed my direction. A shot sounded from above me and took down the beast.

"You're too damn slow," Spoonman growled out while finding a place to laugh in between. "Always dependin' on me to help you out. When you ever going to do your own dirty work?"

"Go light the fires, Spoonman!" I screamed out, hoping I'd not been too late in giving the order. It was time to see if my earlier instructions to Seth would work. I had told him to have the walking wounded gather all the brush they could, soak it with lantern oil, and position it all around the outside of the wagons, about fifteen yards out. A trail of gunpowder ran from just ahead of Spoonman's wagon out to the brush, to ignite it. Remembering the creature rolling on the ground trying to put out the embers on it during the first attack, I had figured the fur of the creatures would ignite easily, I hoped the fire to be a real asset to have on our side.

I watched as Spoonman lit the trail of gunpowder and the sparks ran out into the darkness. Within seconds, the entire circle of brush had flames shooting high into the night. Some of the beasts outside of the circle were balking at crossing over. Others, who tried leaping through them, found themselves engulfed in flames. Those already inside the circle, now visible without the cover of darkness, were much easier to pick off with our rifles. The plan had worked well, and the enemy's losses were great. I only wished the fire would have lasted longer than it did. The brush had been quick to ignite but, like always, burned away too fast. The flames soon died away. Without the threat of catching on fire, the beasts rushed forward.

Shots continued to ring out as the attack ensued. Seth had ceased issuing firing orders as random firing was a necessity. The chiefs were sending all the creatures at once.

It hadn't taken the new guards long to get the hang of shooting. I prayed their shots were hitting something. The bodies on the ground indicated some had. From behind me, screams indicated some hadn't.

I shifted around to find one of the creatures had entered our circle and was attacking. Its claws lashed out at one of the wounded men, barely able to stand, and sliced deep into the man's stomach. Blood spurted onto the beast's fur as its jaws found the man's head and crushed it like a grape. I felt like retching as gray brain matter oozed from the sides of the beast's jaws. A bullet from my pistol, followed by a second, stood the monster up straight and tall, mortally wounded. Falling forward, it landed next to the bleeding body of the man it had just murdered.

Another beast entered from the far side of the circle. I watched as Seth rode toward it, firing his rifle. As he let loose with his last shot, another beast burst from between the wagons and leapt upon his back. Seth didn't have a chance. With unspeakable power, the monster ripped its claws through Seth's body, its hand grasping my friend's heart as it exited the front. I aimed and fired. My shot was true—the bullet entering one side of its skull and exiting the other—and the beast fell to the ground. Seth's body, limp and lifeless, had fallen forward and the saddle horn had somehow latched itself into the hole in his chest. I knew I'd never forget the sight of him bouncing about as his horse galloped around the inside of the circle in a panic.

While those in the outer wagons continued to fire on the creatures outside of the circle, more beasts entered our so-called circle of safety. There was chaos as our people were ripped apart, dismembered and disemboweled. Body parts were strewn throughout the camp. Screams of those being attacked knew no age limitations. From the high-pitched shrieks of children, to the deep screams of elderly men, my ears overflowed with their announcements of finding death.

Rising to my feet, a wave of dizziness forced me to gain the support of the wagon's sideboard. My mind demanded I join the melee and fight the best I could, yet my body was absent of strength to do so. I felt the wagon shake violently and heard Spoonman's screams as his rifle fired one last time. A crunching sound followed. I knew a beast had just taken the life of my oldest friend. It would have to pay.

Gathering every ounce of strength, I stumbled to the rear of the wagon while reloading my pistol and readied myself for the beast to appear. Chances were, it would leave Spoonman's wagon and head right into Sarah's.

To save her and Kincaid from the beast, and to reap the vengeance I had to have, I had to shoot accurately. Yes, vengeance would indeed be mine. This was one time God would have to understand he couldn't have it all. He would have to share.

As the beast threw back the canvas and crouched to jump onto Sarah's wagon, I yelled out, "Hey, you bastard!" at the top of my lungs. Its huge head, with its gaping mouth drooling Spoonman's blood, turned my way. Flames roared from my pistol barrel as the gunpowder exploded and sent a bullet soaring toward its target, immediately followed by another. A red hole appeared in the monster's throat as the first bullet entered and traveled up and into the brain. The second bullet followed the first and finished the job. The beast tried to lean forward and slash out with its claws, but had no muscle control to do so. Instead, it flopped to the ground between the wagons.

"Look out!"

I glanced up to see Sarah raising her rifle and aiming behind me. Spinning around, I saw one of the beasts charging. I raised my pistol and fired without aiming. Another shot rang out as the creature landed atop my body, its weight pinning me against the wagon. I had nothing left inside of me to fight it off. I was helpless as its claws raked up and down my back. I knew I was done. This was the moment I would die.

Suddenly, another shot from Sarah's rifle blew its head apart, spraying blood and brains across my face. Instantly, she was by my side, struggling to get the beast off me. Using all her strength, she was somehow able to shift its huge mass over to one side enough for me to be freed. Behind her, I saw yet another beast rushing toward us. Before I could give warning, its exploding head told me a shot from Kincaid had saved both Sarah and me. Before I could shout out a warning, still another creature shot up the side of the wagon and clutched the boy from behind. Sarah reached for her rifle, but it was too late. The beast's huge fingers and claws grabbed her son's head and twisted it from his body. Sarah's screams filled my ears as the beast tossed the body of her son aside and leapt in our direction. She fired as the beast missed her and landed atop me. I was sent flying at a wagon wheel and remember only the loud pop as my head slammed against it.

Chapter Ten

Had it all been a dream?

I woke on the floor of a wagon, as I had the day before. Or, was it the day before? Had I just awakened from the attack in the narrow pass, and dreamed all the rest? I was unsure of what was real and what was fantasy, until I tried to move. In addition to my throbbing arm, I could tell from my wounds that the claws slicing my back had been real, as well. No dream … just reality.

It saddened me.

That would mean I had lost both my trail assistants, Jess and Seth, on this journey. In addition, my oldest friend Spoonman was no longer alive, nor was Kincaid. Sarah may have been killed, as well. There was so much I wanted to know, but found no energy to move to the front of the wagon and ask whoever was driving for the truth. I could only wait for someone to enter and enlighten me.

The hours passed slowly. Again, my injuries sent me into a quandary of agony with every bump. I knew it would be quite some time before healing would be complete, if ever. What was left of the wagon train would hopefully reach California without my guidance.

I wondered how many of those who had started the journey remained alive, yet was afraid to find out.

Finally, I heard a woman's voice halt the horse team. For a moment, I relished in the stillness of the wagon's motions and the relief it allowed my wounds. The front canvas opened and bright sunlight from outside momentarily blinded me. Gradually, the silhouette of a shapely woman appeared.

"So, how are you doing?"

It was Mrs. Ternam. Not only was I shocked, but sickened at knowing her and her husband were driving the wagon in which I was riding. Surely, he hadn't taken command in my absence!

"I need to get into another wagon," I spoke out as loud as I could, surprised to hear only a whisper come from my mouth. "I won't spend another minute in a coward's wagon."

"First, the coward is dead," she began, a slight grin coming to her face. "During last night's attack, I saw him play the same stunt he had before, only this time, he was offering my daughter to one of the creatures. I shot the monster, and then shot my husband. Good riddance to them both!"

I began to see this woman in a new light. The news of Ternam's death had been welcome, but the news of who had done the deed pleased me almost as much. This wagon train experience had brought out her inner strength, a power she hadn't realized before. It gave her enough gumption to do the necessary deed and free herself and her children from the coward's bondage. I was proud of her.

"Now, I expect you want to hear the bad news. I guess it's up to me to fill you in. There are only forty-seven of us left, twenty-four wagons total. Most of us are women. There's only nine men, including yourself, still alive. All have severe injuries. No children made it through. It seems they were a primary target of the creatures. Poor little things … all lying dead and in pieces around the camp at sun-up. I don't think the sight of the pile of them we buried will ever leave my mind. What broke my heart was finding a small little hand we had missed burying … its tiny fingers still clutching a ragdoll. I'm afraid the memory of that will haunt me until the day I die."

Pausing for a second, her face displayed the emotional strain she had undergone. The stress of the events over the last few days had aged us all. Gathering herself, she continued, "We counted almost one hundred dead Indian warriors in and around the camp this morning. I'd say we got most of them who had the ability to shapeshift. We followed your lead from the first night's attack and used the horses to drag them out and into a line, all of them lying straight and with their arms crossed. As we rolled away, there was a band of Indians on horseback, watching us. They could have attacked, but didn't. Maybe they'd had enough. I know I have. We all have. I'm ready to get to California and leave all of this behind."

I knew all of this was hard on her, but I couldn't let her stop now. I had to find out the answer to a question burning my gut. I whispered, "Did Sarah survive?"

Her hazel eyes began to glisten with tears as she forced out the words, "No, both Mrs. Swisher and her son were killed in the attack. We buried them with the rest of the dead. They're all with God, now. I'm sorry."

She rose and left me alone with my thoughts. I felt so guilty over the questions I'd had about Sarah. She had saved my life, in fact, both her and Kincaid had killed creatures who would have torn me to shreds. They had fought hard, only to end up giving their lives for mine. Her love had been true. I had been a fool.

So many emotions to deal with at one time. So many lost. Jess, Seth, Spoonman, Sarah, Kincaid … the list went on and on. With Mrs. Ternam, Vivian, as I later found out her name to be, she had lost her husband as well as all three of her children. Each of us felt the emptiness of those we had loved now being gone. The grief was overwhelming, yet, almost accepted as a fact of life, considering the circumstances.

The loss of one allows full concentration on everything that person meant to you. When there is a loss of many, the grief is spread about so thinly that the sadness either passes faster or destroys you. In the days ahead, I got to know Vivian well. I won't bore you with the details of her life before the wagon train any more than I already have, or of the remainder of our trip to California. I will say that in moments of sharing a disaster, people are sometimes drawn together. As she nursed me back to health, I found her to be a caring and loving person—one not concerned with wealth. She sought only happiness.

Over the last ten years, Vivian and I have a son and daughter to show for our efforts. It's good to see Kincaid and Sarah playing together, and teasing each other, on our farm each day. Watching them kind of helps me believe they'll have a great future, while remembering those who paid the ultimate price to give me a future.

Well, that was my last wagon train ... the "Train of Blood" as I call it. I'd had enough, seen too much, and ached too bad inside from causing the deaths of so many. Yeah, I still blame myself for their deaths. It was my job to get them through and I failed. No excuses.

Yet, I sit here, counting my blessings to be alive, and am thankful to be growing old with Vivian, when so many died so young.

There are times I sit in my rocker and think back to the story I used to tell the children before we hit the trail. I wanted to save their lives. Each time I told it, I tried my best to make it scarier than the last in hopes it would help to keep them alive.

I imagine there will be someone retelling this story one day. I wonder how they will change it to make it scarier.

If they'd have been there, they wouldn't have to change it at all.

The End

About the Author

Richard "R.C." Rumple began his writing career in the middle 1970s. Writing everything from news stories to his daily Rock radio show, he sharpened his skills as a communicator, storyteller, and humorist.

Leaving radio for a career in Stand-Up Comedy, he continued by writing jokes and humorous tales to keep audiences entertained.

Now, as a writer of Horror, he not only uses his past skills to make his stories stand out, but adds new skills with each effort. A writer of several novels, as well as novel sized short story collections, his work is in constant demand for various author anthologies.

10741132R00075

Made in the USA
Monee, IL
02 September 2019